The Absent Past

The Wilscott Trilogy, Volume 1

Susan Quinn

Published by Susan Quinn, 2022.

This is a work of fiction. Similarities to real people, places, or events are entirely coincidental.

THE ABSENT PAST

First edition. February 10, 2022.

ISBN: 979-8201914615

Written by Susan Quinn.

Table of Contents

This book is dedicated to my late husband, Bob. His continued support and overwhelming belief in me were my inspiration to never give up.

Chapter One
Identities

"Wilson, WILSON! Get your ass over here NOW!"

There he is, my editor, screeching his head off, again. That man is going to have a stroke or heart attack one of these days and I'm sure he'll blame me for that too.

"You'd better answer him, Hunter. He's hoppin' mad," Robin pointed toward the office.

"Yeah, I know Robin, but I'm not prepared to see him yet," I leaned back in my chair.

"Look at the vein popping out of his neck, he's practically purple. Jeez, what did you do now?" Robin shook her head.

'He's bitchin' about what I didn't do."

Robin leaned forward and whispered, "Ya mean the interview with that mega movie star?"

"Yeah. There's supposed to be some deep, dark secret and Woolridge thinks I'm gonna waltz in his front door and this guy will tell me his life story; yeah, right. Wish me luck," I started heading for the boss's office.

"You're gonna need it," Robin remarked.

Walking up to his office, I hastily rehearsed what to say to him so he wouldn't question me anymore. I had a crazy idea to worm my way into that pretty boy's world and I didn't need my boss trying to convince me otherwise.

"Yo, Boss, I'm here, where's the fire?" I asked while leaning on the doorframe.

"Up your ass, you don't give me some good news," Woolridge rasped from his chair.

"I can't just walk up to the guy; I'm working an angle. You gotta have some patience," I said spreading my arms.

"What I got is a deadline. This story is hot now. No telling how soon it will cool off. I won't be scooped by every rag in town. I'd be a laughingstock," Woolridge chewed on his stogie so hard I thought he'd break it off in his mouth.

I didn't think it prudent to tell him everyone already thought him a joke, like a cartoon character in the funny papers. I was in enough trouble. Damn these celebrities. Why did the world bow down to them like gods? They're just people.

"Listen Stanley, to get the whole story, I gotta tread lightly. This guy has the paparazzi following him around constantly. He knows how to answer questions without answering," I explained, plopping down onto the old couch in his office.

"You got some kinda plan up your sleeve?" Woolridge squinted.

"Sure do, but it's gotta be timed just right." I sat forward on the couch and stared Woolridge in *The Eye*. " Let me do my job, Boss. I know it's hard sittin' on your hands but there it is."

He sat up in his chair, "How long?"

"How lo- "

"Till you bring in this story."

"I've been staking him out for a week. I got his routine down pat. My plan goes into effect this afternoon. It's Friday and pretty boy leaves the studio early, heads straight to his place in the hills. He has a blow out every weekend. Hundreds of people come and go throughout the weekend. I plan on infiltrating his fortress and gain his trust."

"Mm, not bad, kid," Woolridge bobbed his head up and down. " Go on, don't get caught up in all that Hollywood crap. Get outta here and back to work."

Getting up off the couch, I said, "Thanks, Boss. See ya Monday."

Yeah, I better see a finished article on Elliot Scott."

I shook my head as I walked away; 'kid'. I'm twenty-nine years old and my boss calls me kid! I suppose to him, I am.

As I came out to the bullpen, Robin's jaw dropped. "How did you manage to tame the wild beast?"

"Gave him what he wanted. Hey, have a good weekend, Robin."

"You, as well. I expect a complete report of what you've been up to, after the weekend," Robin smiled.

Hurrying outside, the heat hit me like a blast from a four-alarm fire and I had to slow my pace a bit as I got used to the oppressive temperature. I jumped into my car, leaving my door wide open, I turned the motor over and immediately set the A/C to warp speed and waited until I could breathe easily again. Shutting myself into my personal oven, I took off down the road and pulled into my driveway. I swiftly got out of my car, locked it up, and walked as fast as I could in the heat, to the bus stop. The silver machine came along directly, and I jumped onboard. It only took fifteen minutes to reach my destination; the intersection of Lexington Ave. and North Gardner St. where I waited, half hidden, behind a massive tree for my opportunity to come along.

I did my research. Mr. Scott would be coming along this road any minute driving a 2019 BMW M850i xDrive in Barcelona Blue Metallic. He would be forced to slow down because of the road construction on the southbound lane, making the traffic merge into one lane. I was nervous as hell, but anything for a story.

Catching sight of his car, I had to get into position and be ready to act. Closer, closer still, I hear the low rumble as he's forced to slow down. He's almost here, the brilliant sun has caught the shiny hood. The BMW is coming into my path...Now! I threw myself at the front corner of his car and immediately rolled back away to keep from being run over and started moaning from the side of the road. I wasn't acting, I hurt like a son of a bitch. I really was an idiot, but he stopped. He's coming right towards me.

"Hey! Are you alright? My gosh, I'm so sorry, I swear I didn't see you."

"N-n- no, I'm okay. I musta slipped off the curb, Just, help me up," I had to play it cool.

Placing his hands on my shoulders, he said, "I don't think that's a good idea, you'd better lie still. I'll call 911."

"Oh, no. Please, no hospitals, "holding my hand up, " I, ah, I don't have any insurance, and I can't afford another bill."

"Yo, you guys alright?" asked a heavy-set man hurrying towards them.

"Yeah, I hit him with my car," Mr. Scott returned.

Shaking my head," Not really, I slipped into his car."

"Can I help, call 911?" the heavyset man was concerned.

"He doesn't want to go to the hospital. I'm gonna take him home with me."

"Would that be okay?" Elliot peered down at me. " I've got some people coming over, but we'll find a quiet place for you."

I was imagining my digits fairly flying over the keys on my PC, typing my way to a raise. Man, my leg really did hurt. I scraped it up good.

Squinting up at him in pain, I said, "I don't want to put you out, just get me to the bench over there at the bus stop and I'll be fine."

"Absolutely not. You're coming home with me. I wanna check out those bruises and cuts you got," Elliot said as his face loomed right into mine while helping me up. I had to admit, he was an extremely handsome guy, and a seemingly nice one too.

The road worker helped him get me into his car. "Hey, thanks man. Awfully nice of you to help," I said.

"Just hope you're really okay. Good luck to ya. Um, before you go, you, ah, you look familiar," he pointed towards Scott.

"Elliot Scott, nice to meet you," he said with his arm extended.

The worker took the outstretched hand and replied, "Oh, of course, Gordon Glay, great to meet you. My fifteen-year old's gonna go nuts. Would you mind an autograph?"

"Not at all, I'd be honored. You, ah, gotta piece of paper?"

"I have one. Would you get my bag from the ground?" I pointed. " I'll get you some paper."

Elliot grabbed the bag from the curb and brought it to me. I reached in and grabbed my ever-present notebook and ripped a page out. I fished around in the bag and found a pen. Closing the bag up, I handed the pen and paper to him.

"Thanks, um, I'm sorry, I didn't ask your name," Elliot looked perplexed.

I was prepared for this question. "No problem, my name's Henry, Henry Withers."

Elliot gave me an extra-long look as I introduced myself and it gave me a warm, funny feeling inside. Hard to explain, even to myself; he just made me feel good and embarrassed all at the same time.

"What's your daughter's name, Gordon?"

"Gennifer, with a G."

There was no traffic at the moment, and it seemed to be as silent as a tomb. The only sound was Elliot's pen scribbling on the paper.

"Here ya go."

"Thanks a lot for this, she really will be thrilled, and Daddy can play the hero for the weekend."

After Gordon walked away with his treasure, Elliot walked around and got in the car.

"Are you sure you're okay? I could drive straight to the hospital."

"No, really it's not that bad.. I'm curious and embarrassed to ask, but you're an actor, I take it. Asking for autographs means you're well known, but I'm afraid I don't know who you are."

Elliot sat there, finger poised over the starter and stared at me.

"You honestly don't know who I am?" Elliot asked with his hand on the keys.

"No, I don't. Would you like me to get out of the car now?"

"Are you kidding me? I can't tell you how good it feels to talk with someone who doesn't know me. We could maybe even have an intelligent conversation on anything but my latest movie, or TV stint. This is really great, Henry."

"Okay, but I still would like to know who you are."

"I'll show you a scrapbook when we get to my place. You can look through it while I set up for the party. Of course, the staff will have most of it done. Oh, don't be surprised if there are a couple of people already hanging out."

He turned onto Lexington Ave., and we drove for a bit in silence. He turned into the driveway of a modest looking house, at least from the outside. Walking inside was like walking into another universe.

"This is incredible, Elliot!"

"My parents' bought the property. I grew up in this house and when they passed on, I decided to stay. I do like the house, but only because it once belonged to Mary Tyler Moore."

"Really? That's impressive."

"Come with me and I'll show you how impressive the bathroom is."

I wasn't looking forward to this, it was gonna hurt. "Yeah, okay, right behind you."

The bathroom wasn't simply a place to do your business, it was an experience. Gorgeous marble walls and countertops, huge shower stall and a luscious garden tub with a skylight. The toilet had its own zip code, along with a bidet. Elliot guided me to a red velvet bench and handed me a glass of white wine, which I drank a bit too fast. He instructed me to remove my shirt and pants, which left me extremely vulnerable to outside influences. While I was doing that, Elliot gathered all of the necessary items needed to patch me up.

"Jeez, Henry, you're bruised in a few places. You're damn lucky you weren't seriously hurt."

"Like I said, I somehow slipped on the curbing right onto your car. I'm okay. I'm also grateful that you're letting me stay for the night. I'm feeling really sore right now."

Elliot's scent was intoxicating. He was so close to me, touching me gently with long tapered fingers. I was slowly getting turned on as he ministered to my cuts and scrapes. He looked up at me and my cock began to thicken with desire. His full sensuous lips were distracting enough but add in that damn dimple on his left cheek and perfectly straight, gleaming white teeth framed by satiny smooth honey colored skin, and I was ready to jump him right then and there. Elliot Scott was the closest thing to perfection in male anatomy I'd ever seen.

I had to keep reminding myself of the task at hand. But, actually, getting close to him, *was* the task at hand. If I had a little fun along the way, who was to know, or care?

"I've got the water running for your bubble bath to get rid of all of those sore muscles that are plaguing you."

"Right, could use a hand getting in the tub, you mind?"

"Not at all. Let's stand you up, easy now."

"Ooh, shit that hurts, jeez I can hardly move."

"That's because you sat for so long in one spot. The soak will do you a world of good."

Elliot felt so good up against my bare chest. He held me until I was lowered down into the lavish garden tub. It had huge windows with tropical plants all around and a skylight. I could get used to this. The hot water felt like a large fluffy blanket keeping me toasty warm. I laid my head back on the padded side and was practically asleep before Elliot left the room.

"I'll be back to check on you in a little while, "Elliot whispered as he shut the bathroom door.

MAN, DO I WISH ALL those people weren't downstairs. This guy, Henry, he's hot. Course I feel horrible that I hit him, but like he keeps saying, he slipped into my car, so technically, he hit me not the other way around. Helping him into the tub without taking the next step took every ounce of willpower I possessed.

That combination of ginger hair and steel blue eyes was such a turn-on, and I don't even wanna think about the scruff on his rosy face. I could hear the murmurings of the crowd with an occasional yell or laugh above the din. All these people, the tradition started many years ago, with my parents. It has always been *just the way it is*. Never able to stand the quiet, they always had a houseful around. Considering how it all ended, it was probably thoughts in their own heads they were haunted by and tried to drown out with constant company.

"Hey, there Elliot," Charlie called.

"Where've ya been?" Bob asked.

"Here ya go, Elliot, have a drink," Chynthia offered.

I took the drink from Chynthia and practically inhaled it. It'd been a rough day. I could still feel the car vibrate when Henry slammed into the side of it. That's when this irrational fear seemed to materialize out of thin air. I continued on to the kitchen to make another screwdriver when I stopped dead in my tracks. There was the absolute distinctive scent of marijuana, coming out of my dad's study. Walking through the doorway, I found Wally, Seth, Bonnie, and Trudy sitting on the leather couch where my dad spent most of his time.

"Guys, no one is allowed in here, this room is off-limits. Everyone out, now."

"Hey, man. Don't lose your cool, we're just smokin' a little weed."
"Yeah, Elliot, you need ta chill, have a hit, boy," Wally said.

"You guys know I don't do drugs. C'mon, all of you, out of this room."

"Okay, okay, ya don't have to give us the bum's rush," Bonnie complained.

"I don't have a problem with you smokin' weed in my house, just not in *this* room."

All of my friends knew I was a bit neurotic when it came to my parents, plus besides smoking weed, these four had been drinking heavily for a couple of hours, chances are they wouldn't remember any of this conversation. My perspective is slightly askew because of that handsome man up in my bathtub. I'm so over this party scene, but I can't just go all postal and start screaming for everyone to get out.

There's less of a crowd here tonight, only around fifty. I just hafta bide my time, have a few drinks, and something to eat. Eat, oh man, Henry's probably starved. I gotta fix a plate.

"Henry? How're doin'? I brought some nachos with chili and guacamole. Thought you might be hungry and could use a hand out of the tub."

Seeing Henry lying there with his eyes closed, breathing softly, gave me a warm, fuzzy feeling all over. I'm not understanding these feelings; I've been attracted to many a sweet ass in my time, this was different. This was the whole package, even my heart did flip-flops when I saw this guy. I brought the tray into the bedroom and then went back to him. Sitting on the edge of the tub, I gently shook him. "Henry," I whispered.

"Umm, whoa, hey there. Wow, I was really out of it."

"You sure were," stroking my hand in the tub water, I remarked, "This water is getting cold, let's get you out of there and dried off."

"Sounds, wonderful. I'm, ah, kinda hungry too."

"I bet you are, I brought you some nachos with chili and guacamole."

"Sounds fantastic, thanks. Let's just get me outta here."

I got behind Henry, wrapped my arms around his middle and pulled while he pushed up with his arms and legs. It took a couple of tries, but we finally got him standing up and out of the tub. He was shaking and cold. I wrapped him up in a soft, thick terry robe and guided him into the guest bedroom.

"How are you feeling? Still very sore? Your bruises are actually looking much better."

"Yeah, I don't hurt nearly as much, that hot soak was just the thing. I'll just lie down for a bit and then get outta your way."

"What are ya talkin' about? You're staying here at least for tonight. You need to rest. Don't worry, it's a light mob here. They'll be gone in an hour or two."

"I'm not worried about your guests, Elliot. I just don't want to overstay my welcome. This crazy accident that happened, it wasn't your fault, and I don't want you feeling guilty or obligated to take care of me."

We stared at each other for about ten seconds, then Henry pulled me close and kissed me softly to which I fully responded. A warmth began in my stomach and spread points due south. My body was screaming out: more, more, more, but then my head had to stick its big fat nose into it and countermand my body by shutting down.

"I'm sorry, Henry. I really want to continue, but right now is not good for me. Let's wait until everyone is gone, okay? I need to be downstairs playing host. You need to eat your nachos and rest. I'll be back to you in a while, deal?"

"Deal. You're right about the food, I really am hungry. You go along to your guests, and I'll veg out here."

"Here you are," I said as I handed him the food laden tray. I gave Henry a peck on the cheek and left the room.

AFTER ELLIOT LEFT THE room, I was able to think again. He had a way of clouding up my brain. Sampling the nachos, I discovered I was famished and ate half a plateful. I was still a bit sore, but not too bad. He had furnished me with some clothes, which I decided to take advantage of. We were about the same size; Elliot was a couple of inches taller than I was, but our builds were very similar. I couldn't help but imagine our naked bodies lying side by side. But, for now, I had a job to do. I quickly dressed and snuck out of the guest room, down the hall to what I was assuming was the master bedroom. Carefully opening the door, revealed that I was on the right track. The room had a California King sized bed, a huge chandelier hanging square in the center of the room, an entire wall devoted to closets, and its own bathroom.

I began in the first closet, looking for boxes that would contain papers, journals, newspaper articles and the like. In the fourth shoe box down, I found a few cutouts from a newspaper. Some were articles and two were pictures. One of those depicted, in a five by seven-inch copy, a man and a woman appearing to be in their mid to late twenties. The article stated they had kidnapped, raped, and killed twenty-seven men and women. I couldn't believe what I was reading, and I thought I was going to vomit. I took the pieces and stuffed them into my pockets. I then put the shoe boxes back the way I'd found them, and quietly left the closet and then the bedroom. I listened at the top of the stairs and heard Elliot talking to someone, so I high tailed it back to my room.

I folded all of the newspaper pieces and tucked them inside my wallet. I took another look at the picture with the caption. It was so hard to think this normal looking couple could have performed such heinous crimes. Even their names were benign, Mr. and Mrs. Thomas Benson. Thom and Mary Benson. And something else. What was it I saw? Looking over the picture again I see, yes near the bottom of the picture there's a boy, about 4 years old. The caption introduces him as Johnny Benson. I can't help staring at their faces and wondering, why? Why would an average family turn on humanity? What sickness runs through the mind that can justify any of the atrocities done to those people. How could Mary Benson go along with her husband's cruel, sick ideas. The shock is in the answer to that statement; they had to be her thoughts as well. Mostly, how could either of them think to do such horrid things with a small boy in tow? Wait a min.., wait a minute, could that little boy be Elliot?

As I started for another look at the paper, I heard a muffled noise outside the room and quickly stuffed the article between the mattress and box spring. Elliot's smiling face appeared in the open doorway and that dimple drove me out of my mind!

"How're ya feeling now? Did you get any rest? Everyone has gone home. There's just you and me in the whole place," he said shyly as he saddled up to the bed. I found myself having to crane my neck to see his face clearly.

Before I knew what was happening, he brought his face down until his mouth was on mine. He rimmed my lips with his tongue, slowly at first, then faster and faster until he twisted it into my mouth and played tongue tag. I couldn't help the small moan that erupted from deep down my throat as Elliot began to suck on my tongue, just the tip at first, practically swallowing the entire muscular organ.

I needed more, more of him, all of him. I let his mouth go so that I could kiss his neck and suck there as well. I ran my fingers through his loose curls and went for his shirt. I got it unbuttoned instantly by ripping it open. Buttons went flying in every direction. I opened my eyes to take a peek, and he hadn't even opened his eyes, he just shrugged the shirt off. He then grabbed for mine, which was also his, and pulled it over my head with no damage to the shirt.

Straddling my hips with his knees, he got a perfect perch on top of me where he could basically do whatever he wanted.

"You doin' okay, Henry? Elliot asked as he gently placed his hands on my shoulders."

"Yeah, Elliot, I'm good. You?"

"Perfect, I'm perfect," he breathed.

I gazed up into his deep hazel eyes surrounded by those luscious eyelashes and swore I could see down into his soul. This was a bit disconcerting because he wasn't one hundred percent sure of himself down in there. The nervousness was momentary and replaced with cockiness and desire.

I reached up and slid my arms around Elliot's back and rubbed him up and down his torso while he laid his hands on my chest and began massaging my nipples. He bent down and kissed, sucked and licked his way down my torso and stomach. He undid my belt and tugged at my pants. I hoisted up my ass and yanked my pants down enough for him to dispose of.

Henry's body was perfection. I felt I was staring at Michelangelo's David; I simply couldn't get enough. The biggest difference was that Henry could actually respond as a very hot flesh and blood person. Although, to be fair about it, a statue couldn't leave you or betray you the way a person could. Okay, Elliot, you're going off the deep end here. I took Henry's pants and pulled them all the way off, maybe a bit rougher than I had to be. Henry gave me a look and I saw uncertainty when I did it.

Henry's cock was a thing of beauty. It was one of the most striking parts of his anatomy I had ever seen, I began to stroke gently. This caused an uproar in Henry, and he began to buck and moan.

"Henry, you are so beautiful. I want to see you totally blow, here."

"Ohm, man. Elliot, I, ah, oh you are driving me crazy, OOOOh. I'm not gonna last, I'm gonna come, OH!"

I reached down between us and freed my bulging member. I began pumping both of us together. Henry brought his hand up too and placed his on top of mine and helped me get a rhythm for the two of us. This was incredible, the sensations were overwhelming.

"Elliot, I'm gonna come, any second, OH, ohm, OH SHIT!!!!"

I listened and watched as Henry blew and it sent me over the edge.

"Yeah, Henry I'm coming. Oh, my fuckin' God!!"

I collapsed and stretched out alongside Henry's body. He felt so good; I swear I felt like a pig in shit.

"Henry? You will stay the night, right? You're not gonna jump up and leave, are you?"

"Are you kiddin? No way, I don't think I could move enough to get out the door right now; even if I wanted to, which I don't."

"I'm so glad. I feel great."

"Me too, Elliot. Me too."

Chapter Two
Past Lives

I showed up early the next day for work at *The Eye.* No one was here yet, not even my friend and colleague, Robin Hill; and she was obsessively early, she couldn't help it.

I might as well play 'throw the paperclip into the cup and earn a point for each one; I couldn't help but be distracted. How I ever got out the door with those articles of the Bensons is beyond me. I just hope Elliot was truly asleep and didn't see me grab those papers from under the mattress.

I kept playing that last scene in the bedroom over and over again, like replaying the same scene on the DVR. Elliot was sincere, I didn't pick up an iota of deceit in his entire body. He was so young, maybe he honestly doesn't remember what his parents did.

I took out the articles, read them over again, made notes and then began to research the case. The case was handled by the FBI because the couple had crossed state lines, but also because they were psychopaths who had killed at least five people.

The more I read about these people, the more ill I became. This couple did horrific things to these people. The research I did confirmed there were also male victims. The cop in charge of the case, a Detective Stone, worked for Hollywood Division. He was thirty-two and brash, but completely focused and worked well with the FBI to catch this couple. The whole thing ended in tragedy one rainy, steamy night during the dog days of August in 1997. Mr. and Mrs. Benson were gunned down in front of the HOLLYWOOD sign up on the hill. The FBI and Hollywood police saved the latest victim, nineteen-year-old Charlotte Warner, and the Benson's four-year-old boy, Johnny, was taken into foster care.

"Good morning. This is Hunter Wilson. I'm with the press in LA. I'm looking for Detective Stone."

Hold please.

Yeah, this is Stone.

"Ah, Amos Stone? The detective on the Benson case – 1997?"

No, you're lookin' for my father. He passed away three months ago.

"I'm sorry to hear that, Detective. Was it on the job?"

Um, kinda, he was still working, but was retiring at the end of that week. Instead, he had a major heart attack chasing down a suspect in a back alley.

"So sorry for your loss."

Thank you. What did you want to speak to him about?

"The Benson case. He worked on it until August of 1997. If I came down to the precinct, would I be able to gain access to the files on the Benson case?"

"Who did you say you were, again?"

My name is Hunter Wilson. I work for a rag named *The Eye*. I'm not proud of it, just had to eat while waiting for my big break to the mainstream papers. I stumbled onto this story totally by accident and would love a chance to get to the bottom of it for the Benson's four-year-old son."

I gotta say, my dad always felt the case needed something. I would find him up in the middle of the night with a cup of cocoa and a snickerdoodle or two.

"Hm, my mom used to make them all the time, my all-time favorites."

Look, I'll meet you outside the Griffith Observatory. The benches on the south side. I've got most of the files in my trunk, can you be there in an hour?

"Can we make it two? I was up most of the night. I'd like to go home, shower and change. Plus, I'm on the other side of town, it's gonna take me a good forty minutes to drive there."

Two hours then.

I decided not to mention this to Woolridge, best to keep him in the dark as much as possible.

"What's up with you?"

"Huh? Hi Robin."

"Hi Hunter. I repeat, what's up?"

"I'm meeting with a detective that might be able to get me the files on the story I'm working."

"Great! How's it goin' with you and pretty boy?"

"It's goin'. He seems pretty normal, considering the life of temptation he lives. I got a gut feeling that he honestly doesn't know anything about what went on when he was a kid."

"You make it sound so ominous."

"Yeah, I'll let ya in on the whole story soon. I gotta get home and change before meeting with the detective."

Home. Well, it's home to me. Wonder what Elliot would say if he got a load of this place, talk about old Hollywood. Elliot's the first guy I'd been with in a long time, and per usual, I went to his place. I usually got invited to the other guy's place. That way, I could get out and go home on my terms and didn't have to get stuck with some guy sleeping over.

I spent my money on contacts for stories and a few good pieces of clothing. My father had taught me at a young age that clothes make the man. Finishing getting dressed, I checked the final product out in my full-length mirror and decided I could play this part.

Now I was off to Griffith Park to meet a man that would, hopefully, get me the story I was searching for.

I love this park, I always have. My mom used to take me to the observatory every Saturday, until she died. It was always an awesome experience. Seeing the planets, stars, and constellations was always such a thrill. I hadn't been up here in quite a few years. I'd have to get back to doing that again.

There he was, at least, I assumed that was him. Skinny little guy with a grey fedora, grey tweed suit and bow tie. The wire-rimmed glasses made the outfit. He looked to be about five feet six inches as he stood in front of the wooden bench. I observed him as I made my way closer. He pulled a phone out of his back pocket, and I was close enough to hear him say, "Okay, I'll be right there." I looked up and he had disappeared. I peered around to see just where the little man had gone, when I heard, "Mr. Wilson, is that you?"

Turning back towards the bench, my knees began to buckle, and my heart started racing in my chest. Sitting there before me was, in all actuality, the most handsome creature I'd ever seen. He was at least six foot seven inches, though sitting down, I couldn't be exact. He had skin the color of caramel apples, hair like sunshine with soft ringlets down to his shoulders, along with hazel eyes. He looked like an ancient Aztec sun god.

"Detective Stone?"

"Mr. Wilson, would you mind showing some ID?"

"Of course, and I suppose I should see your ID as well."

"Yeah, here ya go."

After shaking hands and both of us sitting down, Joe slid a very large corrugated box from the side of the bench until it was right between us.

"I gotta tell you, I'm kinda nervous about what I'm gonna find in here," I said, rubbing my palms together.

"So, exactly why are you looking into this case? I mean, this was such a long time ago and the perps were caught, killed actually. The case is closed."

"Yeah, but what about other family members? Do you know anything about the Benson's son? He was only four when his parents were killed."

"Yeah, I believe the boy went into foster care. Why are you asking, do you think the boy is yourself?"

"Me? Oh, no, no, not at all. I've met someone recently and he could be the boy. In fact, it was through this person I was made aware of the Bensons and their story."

"I think it's safe to say we can trust each other. We passed around our credentials; I'm not sensing there's going to be any problem here plus I ran a full check on you as soon as we got off the phone," the detective boasted. " In this box, are copies of everything to do with the Benson case. My dad made extras of everything. This had been up in my family's attic for the last twenty years or so. My Dad used to drag it down sometimes. He was concerned about the boy, wondered what had happened to him. One of the last times he brought it down, I took them to my car. I was intrigued by his obsession and wanted to discover the appeal."

"I see. I'm concerned as to how much the boy had witnessed and remembers. What if the images are suppressed or repressed or whatever? Could it cause a negative imprint on his brain as he gets older?"

"You've done a lot of thinking on this. I would suggest going through all of the files in this box and then go interview some of the people, if they're still around, and get their take on the boy."

"I would imagine after gathering my info, taking the condensed version to a psychiatrist would be prudent as well."

"Hunter, I'd say you've got a good, solid handle on the situation. You take this box and contact me if you have questions and then if you want, we can get together and discuss it."

"Did you want to come with me? We could pick up some sandwiches and bring them back to my place. Interested?"

"It might be a good idea at that. I haven't been through this box in ages. Be kind of nice to be part of helping my dad. Might make him rest easier knowing what became of the boy."

"So, it's a yes?"

"Yes, on one condition."

"And that would be?"

"We get takeout from *Inn-N-Out*. I'm addicted to that place. My treat."

"Okay, sounds great, and thanks."

Hunter picked up the box and the two headed for the cars in the lot.

Hunter indicated his car and Joe took the keys from him and unlocked the trunk.

"I must say your clothes belie your true colors. I suppose you live in a rat-infested hole in the wall."

"I'm not following you."

"Your clothes are practically brand new. I keep expecting to see the price tag sticking out of the buttoned sleeve. Your jeans are right off the rack in the store. In complete opposition, look at this ole' clunker you drive. This car is what, twenty – twenty-five years old? It's about eight shades of grey in various places and if you scraped all the rust off it'd fall apart."

Joe was right, of course, but it still stung to hear him say that out loud. My little Fiat and I had chased down many a story together. Just because I was only four years old when she was made, so what?

"Yeah, I know, it's rated one of the worst cars of 1995, but hey, it's still running, and we've been through hell and back together. My clothes? I'll tell you a story one of these days. My place? No, it's not in Beverly Hills, and no, there are no rats, you can just see for yourself. I'll meet you in the parking lot of the *Inn-N-Out* on Sunset, okay?

"Yeah, that's fine, lead the way."

After receiving our food, I told Joe to just keep following me. I continued on Sunset and pulled into my driveway. It was long and curved up to the old house at the top of the small hill.

"Jeez Louise, you live here?" Joe asked as his hand indicated the huge house.

"Yup, my job lends me some perks and one is learning about people and where they live. I met the owner, and he was lookin' for a trustworthy person to be like a caretaker; oversee the house. He figured if someone was here, the home would less likely be vandalized. We struck a deal over tequila shots one night and I've been here ever since."

"Now, that's quite the story. Do you know who used to live here? I mean it must have been some movie star or someone in the business somehow."

"There's no spooky manservant or a freaky monkey, but I swear sometimes I feel like I walked into a remake of *Sunset Boulevard*. No, I haven't had a chance to look into it. I'm curious, of course, but my other stories have taken precedence, but one of these days I'll do a story on it and dig into the Hollywood past."

"Is there a pool out back? Do you periodically check for William Holden floating in it?"

"Ha, that's funny. No, but maybe I should start. Although checking the pool is part of my duties. Then, if there's a problem, I call the pool cleaning company."

"This is an awesome place. Sorry if I insulted you before. You read about stereotypes in the journalist business all the time."

"Ya mean like the cops hanging out at the doughnut shops?"

"Touché. You grab the box and I'll get the food."

This house I lived in was very old Hollywood circa 1920's. It was ornate, opulent, and seriously over the top, but I hardly noticed it anymore. I took care of it when I was there, but mostly it was a place to hang my hat. I worked so much, I went home to sleep, shower, change, and out the door again.

Joe followed me into the drawing room from the vast foyer.

"Drop the food on that table in front of the couch," I suggested while I placed the corrugated box on the floor next to the coffee table.

"You want a soft drink, coffee, or I know I've got a couple of beers in the fridge too."

"We're gonna be here for quite a while and eating too, I'll have a beer."

"I was thinking the same thing, be right back. Please, make yourself at home. Feel free to poke around in any room. The bathroom is down the long hallway there," I gestured," second door on the left. I'll be just a minute."

Heading back from the kitchen with the beer in tow, my cellphone went off. Looking at the ID, I involuntarily smiled, and my cock twitched just a tad.

"Hello there."

"Hey, Henry. How's your day going?"

"Oh, not bad, kind of busy. And you?"

"Real busy this morning with rehearsals and close up shots and one- overs, but now it's dead and so boring just waiting around while they adjust lighting and change equipment and set up shots and blah, blah, blah."

"Ha, you're bored out of your gourd, and you naturally thought of me."

"Oh, now who's the funny one! I thought of you, cuz you are the least boring part of my life right now."

I heard a bit of shyness in Elliot's voice. I also felt guilty as I turned into the drawing room to deceitfully snoop into his entire life, behind his back with a man that I found physically attractive. What kind of cad was I.

"I'm glad you called, I felt bad leaving like I did this morning, but you were sleeping so peacefully, I just didn't have the heart to wake you and I had to get to the office really early."

"It's okay, I understand. It was a bit disappointing to wake up to an empty bed, but I get it. I've certainly done the same thing more times than I can count. No worries, here. But, um, you wanna come over tonight? Or maybe go out to dinner?"

"Yeah, I'd like that. You wanna meet at a restaurant?"

"Why don't you come over to my place and then we can figure out where to go from there. Is that okay?"

"Sure, what time were you thinking?"

"Well, that's a problem. I'm not gonna be done here until late, like nine-ish. Would that still work for you?"

"Sure. Message me when you leave the studio, and I'll head over to your place then."

"Great, see you later. They're calling me for a scene. Bye for now."

"Bye, Elliot. Have fun playing in the movies!"

I said this last as I sat down on the couch next to Joe. "Friend of yours? If you have plans, I can skedaddle."

"No, that's okay. He's working, I'm not seeing him until after nine tonight. We have plenty of time to go through this box of yours."

"My dad's box," Joe corrected.

"Right, well, I've got the beer, let's eat and start digging into the past."

We set the food out and I removed the cover from the box. I began to get excited the minute I looked inside. It was chock full of file folders, newspaper articles and actual photographs of the principle players.

"These are pictures from one of the crime scenes. This was Lauren Tremaine," Joe said as he pulled papers from the box. "She was twenty-two when the Bensons brutally raped and murdered her. They aren't easy to look at, just to warn you."

"Thanks, through the years, I've seen some pretty horrific things both in pictures and in the flesh, so to speak. I think I can handle these."

I sounded much more confident than I really felt. Truth was, I was terrified to look at pictures of a raped, tortured, and murdered young woman. Taking the stack of pictures Joe handed me, I gingerly held them in both hands, took a deep breath, and forced my eyes down to look upon the very worst of humanity. In fact, I don't believe these people to be human, but rather some kind of monsters that could mutilate another human being like this poor girl.

From the crime scene photos, it was barely discernable whether it was a man or a woman. Her face was beaten to a pulp; bloody, red and swollen. This continued onto the rest of her body. What made me feel like tossing my cookies, was the amount of blood all over the body. This made it obvious that Lauren Tremaine had been alive while being tortured. I hoped with every fiber of my being she'd been unconscious through the ordeal.

"Hunter? You okay over there?" Joe spoke softly.

"Yeah, it's just, you know, it's hard thinking of a young, vibrant life being snuffed out and knowing full well she went through hell before her final release from this earthly world."

"Yes, it is. I feel that I'm sharing this material with the right person. You sound very much like my dad when he would go on about these murders."

Sifting through the files, I was trying to locate the first victim, or at least the first we knew of. Over the next forty minutes or so, Joe and I worked silently, pulling folders from the box and laying them out all over the drawing room floor.

"Do we have a time frame for these murders?" I inquired.

"The information from the police department and the medical examiner's office. suggests a four-year span running from February 14, 1993, until that fateful day August 13, 1997."

"It's obviously tied into Valentine's Day, but there's something else. Stretching my arm out, I said to Joe, "Gimmie that red file over there, would ya?"

"Sure, here ya go."

"Thanks, I know I saw it some... here it is. John Thomas Benson, born January 23, 1993."

"Bingo, that was the trigger for the Benson's spree. After the baby was born, with all of that responsibility, and being psychotic, they started kidnapping women to maybe prove they were more than just tied down to the baby."

"That actually makes sense, Joe. I think this may be the answer we're looking for, or at least a means to finding little Johnny. We need to find the first victim. That person is somewhere in these files."

"I agree, Hunter, they are. We need to look at all of these articles; plenty of newspaper pieces here. Plus, I remember my dad saying the whole thing started in the wintertime. I don't remember much else, but that I do recall."

"I'm thinking we should go through the pictures and start with the ones from the winter of 1992-1993," I said, pointing to the box.

"Makes the most sense, Hunter."

We spent time perusing the yellowed, news of yesterday, mostly checking the dates and faded photographs until Joe yelled, "I found it!"

Jumping up to sit next to him, I said, "Let's see."

"Here, it's in this article. Quite a few pictures too. The paper's dated February 15, 1993, but it happened on the fourteenth. Tina Driscoll aged twenty with long blonde hair was found in a dumpster in a back alley. Ms. Driscoll appeared to have been assaulted as she had multiple bruises on her person. Sexual assault had yet to be determined. This seems to be the first, and it's only about two weeks after the baby was born."

"Here's your father's folder on Tina Driscoll," I held up a manilla folder full of information. "He basically states the same thing we've been saying about the baby being born in direct correlation to their first kill."

"I can't believe the couple was working together on this; it's probably not politically correct, but I still have difficulty thinking of a woman actually enjoying and participating in any of these heinous acts," Joe's face twisted in disgust. " Did she feel threatened in some way? Did her husband say he'd leave her if she didn't go along with it?"

"I don't think so, Joe. In this article here, Mary Benson tells the reporter interviewing her that whoever mutilated and killed, Betsy Webber, did so to keep their relationship alive. Now that's really sick. Plus, we know there were male victims as well. Could be those were Mary's. Maybe they took turns picking out victims."

"Yeah, I think you're right about that. I'm going to the john, excuse me."

I sat quietly with my thoughts while he was out of the room. I couldn't help but obsess over linking John Thomas Benson to Elliot Scott, but I also couldn't help but be excited about seeing him again, tonight. I was amazed how much I missed him when we were apart.

Chapter Three
Also Known As

"Joe, a thought occurred to me."

"Yeah, it occurred to me in the john as well."

"The foster parents!" they chorused.

"Let's check the files from 1995 on, if there are any,." Joe suggested

"Right. Well, it looks like the folders go up to 1996, so let's see what's in this one. Okay, it's got the name and address of the people that gave little Johnny a home."

"So, who were they? What does it say about them, Hunter?"

"The family's name was Sweeney. Owen and Natalie. They had four foster children back in '96: Jack, Toby, Sarah, Millie, and then Johnny was added. A teacher became suspicious when she noticed Jack wore long sleeve shirts and buttoned up to the collar on very warm days in the classroom. She took the twelve-year-old, seventh grade middle school boy to the guidance counselor, Mr. Todd, who had been trained in generations of child abuse.

He found Jack to have all the signs. They went to Toby next. He was in the same school, but a grade lower. Mr. Todd found the same indications on him. The teacher, Ms. LaFontaine, and Mr. Todd went to the local authorities along with the principal, Mrs. Sanders. Social services were called in and the children were taken from the Sweeney's and dispersed to other families. Little Johnny ended up with a Hollywood couple, Jerry and Kiki Scott. They were both two-bit actors doing voice overs and commercials. They weren't famous or rich, but they made a decent living and wanted a child very badly. Kiki had lost four babies in her first three months of pregnancy, and they couldn't go through the heartache and agony of that again. So, they decided to get into the foster program and take it from there. After learning of Johnny's past, they felt that a brand-new start was in order. Kiki had always admired Robert Stack as an actor and fell in love with him as Elliot Ness in the sixties TV show, *The Untouchables* so they re-named Johnny, Elliot Scott and decided to raise him as their own. Your father's report ends with him explaining how the Scotts never spoke of this horror again. They raised Elliot and he grew up raised the show biz way."

"Elliot Scott, as in the Elliot you were talking on the phone with a while ago?

"That'd be the one. You can see why I'm so invested in this thing now. I met him, rather sneakily to get a story and I ended up really liking the guy. I honestly can't write this article and publish it. It could really damage him, and I know it would destroy our relationship."

Ya know, Hunter, I really don't think Elliot knows anything about any of this. I don't think the paparazzi does either. I haven't heard even a whisper of any of this from the media."

"You're right about that, I haven't either. I just had this feeling that there was a secret and started investigating. Now, I, I just don't know what to do."

"About the story, or about Elliot?"

"Huh, both. I don't know him that well, but well enough to know that he's a good guy. He shows no signs of following in his biological parents' footsteps. I have two really big problems. My boss is this stereotypical hard ass newspaperman straight out of the 1930's. He's expecting this juicy expose on Elliot Scott Mega Movie Star.

After learning all of this, and having spent some time with him, I can't do it. I mean, how could I? This isn't like, my mother was from outer space, ya know?"

"Yes, I get it. Can't you just tell your boss you couldn't find anything on Elliot? I get he might squawk for bit, but he'd get over it, right?"

"Not sure about the getting over it part. I've seen him fire someone for misspelling a word in their article. Depends on his mood at any given moment.

"Sounds like you've got a lot to think about."

"Yeah, I have to come up with two different stories explaining what I'm writing about. My boss is expecting a lallapaloosa of a story on Elliot, and Elliot wants to read my stories in the magazine I write for. How can I show him when I'm deceiving him about who I really am?"

"Truthfully, I think Elliot knows the 'real' you. I don't think you could lie about who you really are, you just lied to him about your name, your cover as it were. You've been playing a part, acting. He should be able to relate to that. I think, if you want to continue seeing him, that you sit him down and be perfectly straight with him. Let him know, you started this as just a story, but because you've come to really like and respect him, you want him to know the truth. Then fess up, tell him all that you did. He'll probably be bullshit for a while, but then come around. He might even be a bit flattered."

Joe and I had been working so diligently making copies of certain key reports from his father, we'd abandoned our food. All of a sudden, I heard an awful noise, like some kind of rabid animal.

"Sorry, guess my stomach is protesting being empty. With the horrors my brain has seen, I don't understand it, but there it is," Joe explained just as his stomach betrayed him once more.

"Ha, that's okay, Joe. I was just thinking we needed to heat up our lunch. What time is it, anyway?"

"Almost seven. No wonder I'm hungry."

"I'll take all the food and throw it in the oven. It'll take just a few minutes to pre-heat and warm the food up. If you don't mind, I'm gonna take a shower and change. If the food is ready before I'm out, make yourself at home."

"Sounds great, thanks Hunter. You, uh, think you'll tell Elliot the truth tonight?"

"Gonna try. Can't guarantee I won't chicken out at the last minute, but at least with the proof from the files, I won't feel so much like a parasite."

"Well, you have time now. Seems like it will be harder to tell your boss you won't be writing an expose on Elliot Scott."

"Yeah, I agree with ya. Help me get all the bags to the kitchen so I can get in that shower."

"While we eat, you can tell me that story about your dad you mentioned."

"Sure, I'll be back in a few minutes."

Coming down into the kitchen, I saw that Joe had laid all the food out for us. "Thanks, Joe. This is gonna hit the spot."

"Yeah, I ate half my fries already, ha. So, what's the story with your dad?"

"Oh, right, well, I grew up very much like Audrey Hepburn in that movie *Sabrina*. My parents and I lived over the garage at one of the most prestigious mansions in Hollywood.

My father was the manservant to the Master of the house and my mother was in charge of the entire kitchen staff and had Madam's ear at all times. This family, the Smythe's with a y, were old money. This money was made from the railroads and oil wells, not from the new fad people in show business. The Smythe's were snobs among snobs and had nothing to do with their neighbors from the moving pictures.

My father had a theory about clothes and the way a person was treated by going to a restaurant in his work clothes. He would take me along and tell me to pay careful attention. They would inevitably seat us way in the back, and almost always next to the kitchen. The service would always be extremely slow, and many tables had their orders taken and food brought while we still hadn't been given menus.

During the meal, my father would get up and take me to the Men's room, where he would take out his best three -piece suit from under his coat, change clothes, and had us sneak out through the back door and come around to the front entrance.

He did this with me, four, maybe, five times and it always amazed me. My father, going to the maître 'd in his best suit got us royal treatment, practically. My father would let it continue until they brought the bill, then he would reveal his work clothes. We were often banned from those restaurants but that's okay. My dad's plans of showing me how people judged by their 'covers', really helped to shape the person I became."

"That's an amazing story, Hunter. What about your mom? She must be very proud of you."

"My mom died when I was young, six years old."

"I'm sorry to hear that, what did she die of? She was so young."

"She was in a car accident. I got up one morning and Mom fixed my breakfast, gave me my lunch and kissed me goodbye at the door, just like every school day. She said be safe, learn a lot, and have fun doing it. She stood in the doorway watching me go on my way, same as she always did. Dad picked me up after school, which was unusual. We went over to the La Brea tar pits and he explained that mom was gone. I thought someone had taken her right out of the house. Poor Dad, I must have been tearing his heart apart, asking those idiotic questions when you don't understand what's happening. Where did she go? How long will she be gone? When is she coming back? As I grew older and recalled those conversations, I would try to apologize, but Dad would just put his hand up and tell me not to sweat it.

Her being gone was a fact in my life, I guess I never thought of questioning it. I missed her like crazy at first and would cry myself to sleep every night, but eventually I started to heal."

"Is your dad still around?"

"No, he passed away a little over a year ago. I feel bad cuz we really weren't very close. He felt that I'd sold out for working for *The Eye* and I couldn't make him understand that I was making my own way, until I caught my big break. He also wasn't thrilled I was gay.

"Uhm, I see," replied Joe.

By 7:50 pm I was squeaky clean, had changed my clothes, and had a stuffed belly. Joe had finished up his meal and was getting ready to head out with his dad's records. My copies were in a box sitting on the coffee table.

"Thanks for everything, Joe. I promise to keep you updated on the latest."

"Good, I'm really invested in this whole story now, I need to know how it all turns out. Thank you, Hunter. I'm glad you contacted me about this story. We may be able to really close it up for good, now that we know what happened to little Johnny."

"It's really all because of your dad keeping such fantastic records. I'll let you know how tonight goes and we'll take it from there."

My cellphone chose that particular moment to go off. Joe said a quick goodbye and slipped from my view out the front door. I hurried over to my phone.

"Hello?"

"Hey there. I'm done and on my way home. You wanna meet me there? Or is it too late for you now?"

"No, it's not too late, for me. I'd be happy to meet at your place."

"Good, I'll see you soon, then."

"Right."

I felt strangely uncomfortable at this moment. I couldn't figure if it was because I was lying to Elliot about who he was, or who I was.

I feel like such a fraud every time I hear Elliot call me Henry. What a mess I got myself into, and I am ninety-nine percent sure I'm not going to fess up tonight. I could already feel myself pulling away from that confession. We only had tonight and then Friday when Elliot always went home early to get ready for his weekend bashes. I'll have to do this on Friday, it'll be exactly one week since I *fell* into his life. Perfect time to tell him the truth. Jeez, just thinking of telling him and my palms are all sweaty.

We pulled into his driveway simultaneously. Me from the North, him from the South. So now our cars were parked side by side in front of the bank of garages. I looked over at him and my brain melted. Elliot Scott was arguably the handsomest man on the planet, just looking at that dimple when he smiles, I couldn't help but grin from ear to ear getting out of my car.

"Henry, so good to see you, handsome as ever."

"Me? Huh, you look in a mirror lately?"

We slipped into each other's arms so easily. There was no hesitation, no awkwardness, just two bodies sliding into place. We moved apart just enough to lock lips for an extremely passionate kiss. You'd think we hadn't seen each other in months instead of hours. Searing heat rushing from my wet mouth, straight down into the pit of my stomach, raging southward to my rapidly filling cock.

We rushed into his house and up to the bedroom leaving a telltale trail of clothing behind. We raced up the stairs taking two and three steps at a time, then crashing into each other at the top and kissed to our victory. We managed to get into his room and slammed the door against the world. I shut my brain down with all my secrets and concentrated on Elliot. It was a glorious night and in the heat of the moment, I had no regret; until the day broke into hazy sunshine and I realized once more how I was deceiving this man lying next to me.

I, of course, chickened out and didn't say a word to him about who I really was. I gathered my clothes, following the trail in the opposite direction until I was at the front door. Dressed and somewhat put together, I again left without waking Elliot. I made it to work just in time to be hauled into the bosses' office.

"Wilson, how is that piece coming? I want to see something on it ASAP! You've been screwing around with it long enough. Show me something by the end of the day, understood?"

"I hear ya, but this story is turning out to be much bigger than I could have imagined. I need more time for research."

"How much time?" Woolridge inquired screwing up his face.

"Just a day or two, enough time to get all the facts."

"Don't take too long with those facts. What we want is sensationalism, something to plaster across the front page."

"Mm, yeah, right Boss. Let me get back to work, or it'll never get finished."

I left his office feeling deceitful to him just as I felt it towards Elliot. What was I turning into? I wasn't liking myself very much lately. I've got to tell Elliot the truth, and soon. I knew it wouldn't be tonight, not with the throng of people streaming in and out and coming and going. Possibly, I could tell him in the morning, but how loutish would that be? Spending the night with him and making lo—. There it was, I wasn't having sex, I was making love. I might as well admit it, I was falling in love with Elliot Scott.

My confession would have to wait a couple more days. After all, what could another forty-eight hours hurt.

Chapter Four
The Truth Comes Out

I was in high spirits. Everything was right in my world, and I was hoping it would stay this way, at least for a while. It was crazy, I barely knew Henry, but I couldn't help my face lighting up whenever I thought of him.

I was zipping along the highway on my way home from work. I'm so glad it's Friday, time to party!

I was listening to the radio and singing off-key to the songs when I heard the unmistakable boyfriend ring. I answered the phone, through my steering wheel.

"Hello, you."

"Hey, hot stuff."

"What's up?"

"Not a whole lot. We gotta wait for a rewrite to come in before printing, so I'm gonna be about a half hour late. Don't have too much fun without me, k?"

"Alright, thanks for letting me know. That was really very nice of you. I'll see ya soon then. Bye.'

I veered around the curve and pulled into my driveway just as about fourteen or fifteen people all tumbled out of my house. Bud and Chris ran over to the car.

"Hey, Elliot. Nobody brought any beer; can you go over to the corner store and get some? Me n' Chris'll come with ya."

"Sure, hop in. Hey, when Henry gets here, tell 'em where I went, okay?"

"Will do. Just get that beer back here," Ronnie yelled from somewhere in the house.

We grabbed two thirty packs of Corona and headed for the cashiers. Standing in line, I absently watched the other patrons. Chris was busy looking at a couple of girls in the next row over and Bud picked up one of those rags where everyone is having alien babies, and the celebrities are all having sex with each other. Bud was holding one called *The Eye*. Their motto read: Keeping Our Eye on the Public.

His face suddenly contorted as if he had been struck by a severe migraine.

"Hey, Bud? You okay, there?"

"Um, Elliot, who does this look like?"

Holding the paper up in my face, I got a good look at the picture Bud was indicating. It was obvious who it was, and I said so.

"That's easy, Bud. It's Henry." Of course, as soon as the words were out of my mouth, I felt all the blood drain from my face. What was I saying? Henry? MY Henry? Impossible!

Bud edged closer to me with the tabloid, and I took it from him as if it were a priceless Grecian vase. Staring back at me was the face of the guy I'd been sleeping with, but the name under it read Hunter Wilson.

My phone chose that exact moment to go off and naturally, it was Henry.

"I can't, Chris, I can't answer the phone. Here, you guys, take my debit card and buy the beer, I gotta get some air."

By the time I got to the car, I was in a full-blown panic attack. I couldn't catch my breath; my extremities were tingling; I was dizzy and could barely stand up and my head was pounding. I climbed into the back seat and curled up into a small ball. I was shaking uncontrollably and sweating profusely. Chris and Bud got in and Chris drove us home.

I kept my eyes glued shut and tried to keep my head empty for the ride home.

Chris parked the car and I heard, voices, angry voices, outside of my car. The car door by my head then opened. "Elliot? Elliot, please look at me. Can you hear me?"

Oh yeah, I could hear him, that voice that made me quiver merely hours ago, now felt like a knife plunging into my vital organs.

"Guys, what's going on?" Henry asked again.

"He's having a panic attack. Bud, show him the paper."

"Here, *Henry,* this is what's wrong with Elliot," Bud snarled.

I lifted my head up just enough to watch Henry's face as the full weight of the situation hit him like a ton of bricks.

His face was becoming as red as his hair, and he had to grab onto the car. Bud opened the car door and helped him in, so there we were staring at each other.

"Ell –"

"Shut the fuck up."

"Look, I kn-"

"I said SHUT- THE- FUCK- UP and get out of my car."

"I'll leave for now, but I'll be back, later," Henry said as he jumped quickly out of my car.

I instantly grabbed a plastic bag from the floor of the car and vomited.

"Elliot? Elliot? You okay? Here I'll sit with you. Let's take a few minutes before going in," Chris said.

Bud had shut off the engine and we sat in the driveway until I felt I could manage getting out of the car.

I continued to stare after Elliot's BMW in my rearview mirror. I was still in shock. Obviously, I knew I would get caught eventually, but things were going along so well, guess I was only foolin' myself.

Gut punched, that's how I felt. I could barely breathe. I'd been wandering around aimlessly for hours. Nothin' left to do, but head to the office and talk to Woolridge.

"You wanna run that past me, one more time, Wilson?"

"I said the 'honeymoon' is now over. He's figured out who I really am and why I'm there. He threw me out."

"How close are you to getting me the story?"

"Boss, it's only been a week. I had just scratched the surface with those pictures and articles. Now I've got –."

"Shit, you've got fuckin' shit, yes?"

"Ah, well, yeah, Boss. I got shit."

"Out! Go clean your desk out right now and don't let the fuckin' door hit you on the way out.. I'll give you twenty minutes before I call security and have your ass hauled out of here."

Leaving Woolridge's office, the reality of the day was finally beginning to hit me. Back at my desk, Robin rushed over and sat down, right next to me.

"Hey, my friend. How're ya doin'?"

"Hey, Robin, I've been better, that's for sure."

"What did Bossman say?"

"I have about six minutes left to get out before he calls security."

"Oh, sweetie, I'm so sorry. You wanna order Chinese and watch bad movies all night?"

"You're the best, Robin Hill," I said, and I craned my neck over and kissed her on the cheek.

"I've got everything packed up, let's get outta here."

"Great, I'll take these two bags for you," Robin said as she took two small plastic bags and brought them down to her car.

We got to her apartment building about the same time and parked. We climbed the two flights of stairs and entered her place. I immediately slumped into one of the easy chairs.

"How about a drink, Hunt?"

"Yeah, I'll take a beer, if you have any."

"Sure, and then you can tell me why Woolridge canned you."

"Elliot found out who I really am, and he kicked me out. Oh, Robin, if you could've seen his face, how hurt he was. I shattered his entire universe. Knowing I'm responsible is making me physically ill."

"I'm sorry, Hunter. I could see how much you cared for him. I watched you come to work every day with a smile on your face and a little skip in your walk. You've been floating on Cloud Nine, my friend."

I sat and listened with amazement. I had no idea I was acting this way, but it was making perfect sense.

"You know what I realized earlier, and you have just confirmed it."

"What's that?"

"I'm falling in love with Elliot."

A small, knowing smile crept across Robin's lips. Taking my hand gently in hers, she said, "Yes I know. So, what about Woolridge?"

"I told him there was no story because Elliot found out who I was, but to be honest, I wasn't going to do the story anyway. I couldn't do that to him. He has no idea of his biological family and I sure as hell won't be the one to splash it all over the tabloids."

"And for that, he fired you. Not really a big surprise, knowing him. Ya know, Hunter, this might be a blessing in disguise."

"What d'ya mean?"

"You would've stayed working for that sleazy rag for the rest of your life and never have taken a chance at a real newspaper. Well, you're out from under Woolridge and his paper, so go dust off your resumes and be brilliant!"

"Robin, you always know just the right thing to say to make me feel ten feet tall. Thank you, darlin'. If I wasn't gay," Hunter trailed off with a whimsical smile on his lips.

"Yeah, yeah, I've heard it all before. Let's order Chinese and watch bad movies until we fall asleep on the couch. You can even paint my toenails, how's that?"

"Sure, Robin. Hey, make sure you order that sweet and sour chicken we got last time. That was so good."

"Already highlighted all our favorites. Good thinking about the chicken though, I got it under control. What movie do you want to watch?"

"Something really funny, so I can forget my problems, at least for a little while."

I woke up and tried to figure out where I was and how I got there. At that moment, Robin moved her arm, and it all came flooding back to me. Robin and I had watched several comedies until we couldn't keep our eyes open and fell asleep together on the couch. There were Chinese food cartons littering the coffee table in front of me. I picked them all up and threw them in the trash, relived myself in the bathroom and seeing it was almost three in the morning, kissed Robin's forehead, and covered her with the quilt she always kept on the back of the couch. Her grandmother had made it and Robin always displayed it to honor the woman she admired.

I wrote Robin a brief note and quietly left the apartment. I headed straight to my car, got in and took off for home. Once I was in my sanctuary, my mind continually played scenes of Elliot's face. I was a wreak. I got to my room, stripped down and took a long hot shower, before crawling between the sheets, intending to never leave my bed again.

"I WANT EVERYONE OUT of my house. Understood?"

"Yeah, me and Chris, we understand, right?" Bud replied.

"Absolutely, we do," Chris agreed.

"I'm going in through the side door and straight to my room. Don't say anything, just get rid of 'em."

"Got it, we'll take care of everything," Chris assured.

I didn't know how I was going to make it to my house, let alone the rest of my life without Henry, but I had to. I still can't believe I fell for his routine, although I have to admit, it was a clever plan.

I quietly went through the side entrance and tiptoed up the back staircase to my room. I could hear quite the ruckus downstairs, but frankly I didn't give a shit. I took a very long, hot shower and climbed into bed. Problem was, I couldn't close my eyes without seeing Henry floating in front of me. It was hours before I finally fell asleep, and I had to be up for a five-a.m. call.

Chapter Five
Blindsided

"Elliot, Elliot! ELLIOT!!"

"Yeah?"

"Look, Scott, I need your head in the scene, got it? Let me know when you're ready to work, or if I need to move on to another scene till, you're invested, okay?"

"Yeah, yeah, alright I hear ya already. Maybe if I had a decent script to work with, I'd be able to concentrate!"

"You gotta stick up your ass? Yank it out, break it off, or ignore it. Just stop blaming me and everyone else around here for your ineptitude," Harold spat out between his clenched jaws where that cheap, smelly ole' cigar logged between his yellowing teeth.

"I'm not runnin' a fuckin' daycare around here. Youse people are supposed to be adults. I'm friggin' sick of playin' babysitter around here. Now, I need everyone to get outta my sight and take your marks. GO!"

"Jeez, pretentious director." As I'm headed towards my mark on the set, I hear, "Elliot, get over here."

Great, another county heard from. My manager, Julius Barrows, has consistently bad timing. He's always showing up on my set, scrounging for clients, and other things I don't want to know about. He's either here to hit me up for an advance, or he's got some whacko idea he wants me to be a part of.

"Hey, Jules, I can't really talk right now. Harold is on the warpath, and I've got a scene to do."

"Yeah, no problem. I was just gonna invite myself over to your place this weekend. Haven't been to a good bash in weeks."

"Sorry, I'm not having anyone over this week-end, or any time in the near or distant future."

"You're puttin' me on, right?"

"Nope."

"Excuse me, MR. Scott. Are you still working here?"

"Yes, sir, coming. Jules, I can't talk now."

"Okay, I'll text you."

As my co-star and I took our places, we heard that grating voice once more.

"If you two are finished with your social obligations, maybe we can finish this scene sometime before midnight."

"We're on our marks and ready," Shawn barked back.

My co-star, Shawn Weston was young and impetuous. He didn't take shit from anyone. He wasn't the typical narcissistic actor; he knew who he was and was comfortable being himself. We hit it off right away and complimented each other in all our scenes. They used to call that 'having great chemistry', not sure what they call it nowadays, but it works for us.

Standing there waiting to begin my lines, someone walked by reading that rag, *The Eye,* and I was transported instantly to the corner store. My head started reeling as a kaleidoscope of images pulsated in my brain. I was having trouble catching my breath and I thought for sure I was going to pass out right there on my mark.

Then I heard someone's voice calling from way off somewhere, 'Elliot. I came out of it and was immediately embarrassed as I realized everyone had gathered around to see what the matter was. Shawn was right by my side.

"Elliot? Elliot you okay? Should we call an ambulance?"

"No, no I'm alright, really. Just got a little dizzy is all. Everyone, please, I'm fine."

"Can everyone go back to their jobs, and can you bigshot Hollywood actors get back on your marks and ready to go? This is costing me fuckin' money!"

"Hey, ease up, Harold. Elliot needs a minute."

"Oh, so sorry Weston. Of course, Scott needs a minute so let's just shut down all production until he's better," the weasel director spat out.

"Okay, you guys, Shawn, Harold, I'm fine. Let's just get on with the scene."

We started the dialog and I messed it up so many times, it was nearly dark, and the scene still hadn't been finished. Everyone was getting tired, frustrated and angry with me. Even Shawn had about had it.

"I'm sorry, okay? I just can't get my head around this scene today. I don't know what else to do."

"You could try saying your lines correctly," my insensitive director retorted.

"Oh, yeah, Hovis, cuz sarcasm works so well, I should be able to spout my lines out now! What the fuck, don't you understand anything? I can't do this right now. I need to take a break, and everyone needs to go home and try this again tomorrow."

" Hey, look here, ACTOR, I'm in charge here and I'll tell everyone when they can leave and when they have to stay. YOU need to get your head back in the game and DO THIS SCENE. You're an actor, so act! You got personal problems, leave 'em in the bedroom."

Something snapped inside of me and before I could think about it, I lunged at him. Taken by surprise, Harold went down like a sack of potatoes. I landed on top of him and proceeded to punch the shit out of his face.

It happened so fast, it took the rest of the crew a few seconds to catch up to what was going on and when it did, I had multiple hands and arms pulling me off Hovis. His face looked like a piece of pulverized hamburger. He was wheezing and breathing hard. His left eye was completely closed, but he still managed to sit up and look right at me.

"You are so fuckin' fired, Scott. Get the fuck off my set and off this lot. You got five minutes, and I'm being generous here. Call security, if Elliot Scott is so much as seen on this set, blow his fucking head off!"

I knew he was serious and took off for my car with a purposeful step.

"Elliot! Elliot, wait up."

I turned to find Shawn jogging towards me. "Hey, you shouldn't be talking to me, you'll get hit in the crossfire."

"Nah, he won't get rid of both of us, I just wanted you to know I understand what you're going through. Been there myself and it's gonna take time. Don't beat yourself up over what you're feeling right now. Just go with it. Take some time to let it hurt and then you'll begin to heal."

"Thanks, Shawn. Those are very wise words, and I'll take them to heart. You better get back there now. Good luck with the picture."

"Thanks, best of luck to you."

We shook hands and he started back to the set, and I jumped in my car and took off. I had no idea where I was going but it had to be out of town. As I was driving, I realized I was headed for the beach. I parked and started walking. Sitting there watching the waves lick the shore and turn the sand to mud, I was reminded how big the world was and I was just a tiny speck in it. Made my problems seem much smaller than they were an hour ago. I was still hurting, but at least I was able to breathe.

Now I need to figure out my next move with Henry. I'm wondering if I should at least listen to him. I need to know what he's been after. Think it's time I give him a call. I will do that, maybe tomorrow. For now, I'm gonna sit here and watch the sunset, maybe even stay the night.

I TOSSED AND TURNED all night long and was up and showered by four a.m. I wasn't hungry but thought doing somewhat of my normal routine would at least make me feel human. Many times, while working in the middle of the night, I would stop by this diner that served the best eggs in the neighborhood. I decided to take a jog and stop by the place on my way home.

I was nearly there and cut through the alley next to the street where my favorite diner was located so I could come in through the back door. As I passed by a trash container, I heard noises and felt rather than saw movement. I hurried my pace as I quickly glanced behind me. Not seeing anything, I chuckled to myself. *C'mon Wilson, you're being paranoid.* Getting past the receptacle, I breathed a little easier and slowed my walk down a bit. I was merely yards from the diner when suddenly a figure jumped straight out in front of me. He was dressed all in black with a hoodie covering his head and much of his face. He was carrying something in his right hand, looked like a stick of some sort. He just stood there silently staring at me. I, of course, stopped and stared back. He was built, rather muscle bound and at least six foot three inches.

"Hey, man. I'm just cutting through to get to the diner right there. I'm not looking for any trouble. If I trespassed on your turf, I'm sorry, man. I promise I won't come through this way again."

As I was talking to him, I saw two more guys, dressed the same way, come from either side of me. Each of them had the same sticks. I realized then; they were long pieces of pipe. None of them said a word but began inching closer to me.

The first blow to my back knocked me straight to the ground. I couldn't breathe, couldn't move. Never in my life had I felt pain like that. I was on my knees, trying to get my breath and my wits together when the second blow got me right across the chest. I remember falling backwards with my legs caught under me. That's when I heard my ankle bone snap along with a couple of ribs. I was in agony from only two hits when they all looked at each other and descended on me all at once. I rolled over and protected my head as best I could, but it still got hit. I was going numb when I heard, somewhere off in the distance, someone yelling. The trio ceased hitting me and backed up quickly and ran away as silently as they had appeared.

Senor Gomez began running over to me. "Don't move, boy. Stay still. I have mi esposa calling the police."

"I d-d-don't know who they were," I managed to croak out.

"Don't worry, son. We'll take good care of you."

"Pedro, the police are coming, and they are sending an ambulance. How is the dear boy?"

"He is not good, Marisol. Go get a blanket, he's going into shock."

"Elena is bringing one now."

I could hear them talking, but I was shaking so much, and it hurt everywhere. I wasn't able to move at all. I knew things were broken, but I couldn't determine where the pain was located. I just hurt everywhere. I did manage to say one thing. "Please call Robin Hill. Her number is in my phone."

I was trying to get my phone from my back pocket and Pedro reached over and got it for me. "I will call her for you. What is your name, son? I know you eat here a lot, but we've never introduced ourselves."

"My name is Hunter Wilson. Let Robin know what happened and what hospital I'm going to." As the words left my bleeding mouth, I heard the unmistakable sirens of the police and the rescue close behind with an engine.

I was vaguely aware of being poked and prodded, along with taking vitals and IV's started before loading me onto a gurney and into the rescue squad. I heard Mr. Gomez talking to the police and telling his perspective of the incident and knew I would have to do the same at the hospital. It was a short ride to the General Hospital. Once there, the paramedics gave their report to the intern in the ER as I was handed off.

"My name is Dr. White. Can you tell me your name?"

"Wilson, Hunter Wilson."

"All right, Mr. Wilson. Do you remember what happened to you?"

"I was, ugh, attacked in an alley by three guys with lead p p pipes. Oh, doc, that really hurts."

"Sorry, I need to assess the damage. You've got quite a few broken bones from what I can see. Nurse, we need to get X-ray down here stat."

"Yes, doctor, right away."

I watched the nurse scurry over to the phone to call them, but I was only able to see part of her.

"Dr. White? What's wrong with my eyes? I can only partially see."

"You were hit on the left side of your face, your left eye is swollen and completely closed. I want X-rays before I try to open it."

I heard, rather than saw the nurses cut off all of my clothes and quickly slip a johnnie onto my bruised and broken body. Lying there, I heard a familiar voice and knew that Mr. Gomez was true to his word and called Robin.

"Hunter?" I heard her whisper.

"Come here, Robin. It's okay if you can stand to look at me."

"Oh, baby, what happened? Oh my God, look at you! Mr. Gomez told me you had been hurt in the alley by the diner, but I had no idea it was this bad. Who did this to you, Hunt?"

"I have no fuckin' idea, Robin. There were three of them and they all had lead pipes."

"I'm sorry, Miss, you'll have to leave for a bit, we're ready for his X-rays."

"Of course, doctor. Hunt, I'll be right outside, and I'll come back in as soon as they'll let me. Want me to call Woolridge and tell him what happened?"

"I'd rather you didn't, let's keep this between us, okay?"

"Sure, okay, see you in a bit."

"Elliot, are you gonna mope around all friggin' day? We got better things we could be doin'. Why don't we call the gang and have a bash?"

"Look, Dev, I'm in no mood to party. You guys wanna party? Go to somebody else's house. I'm just gonna sit here and veg."

"Elliot where is everyone?" my disgruntled manager fumed.

"Oh, jeez, that's all I need. Look Julius, I'm not having any fuckin' parties. Why don't you take Dev and go back to your place and start your own party. I have a lot of thinking to do and I need to be alone."

"Yeah, sure, Elliot. Word of advice? call him. Have it out with him and clear the air. Maybe you get back together, maybe you don't, but at least you'll have closure. You can't keep going like this. You've already lost a movie. You don't want to get a reputation of being difficult or impossible to work with. You do and you'll be washed up in this town."

"I'm listening, Jules. I know I gotta do something soon. I had made up my mind last night to call him, but in the light of day, I simply chickened out. Give me a little while to get my thoughts together and I'll do it."

"Good, Dev and I will take off and leave you to your thinking. Let's go," Jules laid his palm firmly on Dev's back and pushed. " I'll buy us some lunch."

"Hey, sounds good, Julius. Take care, Elliot. See ya later."

"Yeah, see ya."

I sat for a while by the pool and replayed every moment with Henry, like a Saturday matinee. Remembering the look on his face when we'd make love, that couldn't have all been faked. He must have felt something towards me. I needed to find out for sure. Picking my phone up, I pressed number one on my speed dial. I was expecting either voicemail, continuous ringing, or Henry's voice as he actually picked up the call. What I got, through me totally off balance.

"Hello, this is Hunter Wilson's phone. My name is Robin Hill. Elliot is that you?"

"Ah, um, yeah. I'm sorry, who are you and why are you answering Hen—Hunter's phone?"

"There's no easy way to tell you so I'll just say it. Hunter was beaten to a pulp in an alley. He's in the ER right now. They are assessing his injuries and he may have to have surgery. Hunter and I work together and are very good friends. Elliot? Are you still there?"

"Oh God, when did this happen?"

"About forty minutes ago now, or at least that's when they called me."

"What hospital is he in?"

"General Hospital."

"I'll be right over, give me a half hour to get through the traffic."

"Just ask at the desk in the ER. He's in cubicle four."

"Thanks."

...

Robin got back to my room in time to meet Joe. "Robin, this is Detective Joe Stone. He's the one that helped me with that little project I've been working on."

"Pleased to meet you, Detective. Are you working on Hunter's beating?"

"Nice to meet you too, Robin. Yes, I've been assigned the case because I volunteered for it and call me Joe, please.

"Hunter is still having tests done and as you can see, he's not in the best shape, so if you could go easy with him—"

"Robin, I'm okay enough to answer some questions. It just hurts to breathe, and talk, and move, that's all."

"I'll be as quick as I possibly can. Now, Hunter, did you get a look at them?"

"No, they were all dressed in black and wore hoodies that covered most of the face. It seemed to me they had blackened their faces as well."

"How many were there?"

"There were three of them. They came out from behind the dumpster and each of them carried a lead pipe."

"You didn't have a chance of defending yourself. You're lucky to be alive."

"I did manage to shield my head a few times when they attacked me all at once."

"What is the damage? I mean, physically, how many injuries?"

"I don't really know; Robin did the doctor say anything to you?"

"Yes, he told me everything since I hold your health proxy. I'm not sure you're really up to hearing all of this."

"It's okay. I know that I have a lot of injuries, just tell me how bad it is."

"Okay, my friend. The orbital bone in your left eye is completely shattered, which means at least one surgery, maybe more. You have four broken ribs and a punctured lung. That's why you're having trouble breathing and you got a tube sticking out of your chest. The doctor has ordered an ultrasound to check for internal damage. Your right kneecap is smashed, and your left ankle has two broken bones: the tibia and the fibula."

Hearing a gasp, I looked up to see Elliot standing in the doorway. His hand was over his mouth, and he was getting paler by the second.

"Elliot, you okay?"

"Ah, yeah, yeah, I'm fine. I can't believe what I just heard. Who did this to you, Henry?"

"Don't know, but how'd you know I was here?"

Elliot glanced over at Robin, and I knew. "You called him?"

"No, he called me, or rather he called your cell and I had it on me, so I answered."

"You called me?" Despite the gravity of the situation, my heart did a happy dance at this news.

"Yeah, I, well we can talk about that another time. Henry I am so sorry this happened to you. Do you know who it was?"

"No, we were just discussing that, oh Elliot this is Detective Joe Stone and I guess you sorta know Robin."

"Elliot, nice to meet you," Joe smiled as he held out his hand.

"You, too. I hope you get the bastard that did this to him."

"Bastards," injected Robin. "There were three of them with lead pipes."

Doctor White chose just that moment to walk in. "I need everyone to clear out. Mr. Wilson needs to rest, and we're about to do more testing."

"What kind of tests, Doc? I'm starting to really hurt."

"We'll get you more pain medication. I'm going to start with an ultrasound to check out your belly. You've got some nasty bruising straight across your mid-section and I want to rule out internal damage."

"We'll be back later on, Hunter," Robin said as she bent to kiss my forehead.

"I'm going to get right on this. Hopefully, they left some clues behind. Doctor, I assume you took precautions with his clothes as you cut them off," Joe said cautiously.

"Yes, we followed protocol. His clothes are with Nurse Briggs, she is where the chain of evidence stopped."

"Great. I'll go take care of that. I'll be back to see you, Hunter. Take it easy and do what the doctors say."

"I will and keep me informed on the investigation."

"I'm gonna be in the waiting room. I'll come back in before they take you to a room," Elliot said uneasily.

"Thanks for coming, and we do need to talk," I said pointedly.

"Yes, we do, but right now you need to focus on healing."

"I'll see you in a bit."

As Elliot disappeared from my view, out of my good eye, I felt a strange sense of loss. I suddenly felt very alone.

"Now, Mr. Wilson, let's talk about the next step."

"Yes, please, Doc. I need to know everything and call me Hunter."

"Very well, Hunter. First, I want you to know we have sent for an eye specialist. Your optic bone has been shattered and will need to be replaced. That will all happen once the specialist goes over the X-rays, tests, and can examine you to decide on the best course to take. In the meantime, like right now, you are going up to the O.R. to re-inflate your lung, replace your kneecap, and set your ankle. The ankle will probably need plates and screws or pins, perhaps both. I know this is a lot to take in, but do you have any questions?"

"What are you replacing my kneecap with?"

"An artificial one, don't worry, we don't take kneecaps from people!"

"No, I didn't think so, well, maybe just for a second or two."

"Nurse Briggs will be coming in a few minutes to give a sedative. That will relax you as we bring you up to the O.R."

"May I see my friends for a sec before I go?" I asked because the nurse was already here to give me the sedative.

"Of course, I'll go get them."

"Thanks, Doc."

I was already getting sleepy when Robin and Elliot came back into my cubicle. Seeing them standing there together seemed very right to me. I felt better, not so alone, with them here.

"Doctor White explained what was happening. Don't worry, they can rebuild you. You're gonna come back faster and stronger than you ever were," teased Robin.

"Oh, don't make me laugh, I hurt everywhere. They gave me something to relax me and I think it's working. I'm really sleepy," I said as I began to yawn.

"We can only stay a second. Henry, I want you to know how sorry I am for the horrible things I said to you. We can have a long talk when you're feeling better."

"Yeah, I'm sorry for deceiving *YAWN* excuse me, deceiving you. I want you to know, I was never going to turn in the story."

"He's telling you the truth, Elliot. He was fired yesterday because he wouldn't do the story," Robin interjected.

"You got fired? Yesterday? Wow, small world. I got thrown off the movie set yesterday. The director basically told me to go fuck myself and he'd see me in Hell before he'd hire me for another one of his movies."

"Why did they fire you?"

"We'll talk all about it later." As Elliot spoke, the orderlies showed up with the gurney to take me.

Robin reached over and gave me another kiss on my forehead. Elliot stood there, not sure what to do. Then he leaned over and kissed me while holding my hand. It felt like coming home.

"We'll see you when you get back," they both said in unison.

I was wheeled away watching the two most important people in my life become smaller and smaller until they were mere dots in the distance. I felt exhilarated for about a half a second, then I drifted off.

Chapter Six
A Shocking Discovery

As I watched Henry being wheeled away, I had the strangest feeling of Deja Vue. It only lasted a few seconds, but there it was.

"Are you going to stay or go home? I can call you when he's out of surgery."

It took me a minute to realize Robin was talking to me. "No, I think I'll just stay here, if you don't mind, that is."

"Absolutely not. To tell you the truth, I'd enjoy the company and I won't be so worried about Hunter."

"Hunter. I can't get used to that name," I said, shaking my head. "He'll always be Henry to me. I'll try to call him Hunter, but no guarantees."

"I honestly don't think he minds in the least. You called him Henry at least three times today and he never corrected you. I know things became strained between the two of you because Hunter lied about who he was and met you under false pretenses, but he confides in me and I shouldn't be telling you this, he'd kill me if he knew," Robin rolled her eyes, " but you mean a great deal to him and he never did or would write anything about you in *The Eye*, or anywhere else."

"Wow, that's a lot to take in. He's important to me as well and that's why it hurt so much to find out Henry wasn't really Henry. What I really don't get is what story could he have possibly found on me?

There's nothing in my life that I'm aware of that could be sensational enough to put in one of those rags."

"Well, we'll leave the explaining up to him, when he's feeling better."

"Mm, you're right. You want some coffee? There's a machine right down the hall."

"Sure, no sugar, light on the cream, thanks," Robin responded with a smile.

I walked down to the vending machines and got two coffees. I ventured down here more for the walking part than the coffee. I was nervous about Henry of course, but it was more than his operations. Our relationship began with lies and I was afraid we wouldn't be able to ever really recover . I found Robin to be thoughtful and kind. She continued to make me feel better as I returned with the coffee.

"Hey, Elliot, Hunter's gonna be fine. He's tough, made from hearty stock. He'll be back on his feet in no time."

"Thanks, I think I really needed to hear that. The police have no leads as to who did this?"

"Not that I've heard, but the detective did just leave a little while ago. I'm sure they're doing all kinds of forensic investigating."

"You learn about that on your job?"

"NCIS," giggled Robin.

We both laughed then which helped to break the tension. As positive as she was being, I could tell Robin was as scared as I was. It didn't take long to figure out that Robin was a tremendous friend.

We'd been sitting there for about an hour when my pals Chris and Bud wandered in.

"Hey, guys. It's nice of you to come down here, but there's not much to do but wait. Robin, these are my friends Chris and Bud, guys this is Henry's friend Robin."

They all said hello and shook hands, but something was off. The guys were acting squirrely, and Robin picked up on it right away.

"Something goin' on that I should know about?"

"We can discuss it later," Chris replied. "Yeah, later," Bud mimicked.

I looked from one to the other and knew there was something serious going on.

"C'mon, follow me." I brought them down to an empty conference room I had noticed when I got the coffee. I pulled them both in with me and shut the door.

"All right, spill. I know somethin's up. You both look as guilty as the time you ate the entire pecan pie at my aunt's house, and she scolded you for eating our dessert."

I looked from one to the other, looking like I was at a tennis match. "I'm waiting."

Bud began to speak first. "Well, see, we, ah, well we knew how bad you was feeling after that liar hurt you. So, we, ah, we—"

My heart started to pound out of my chest, and I began sweating. He couldn't be saying what I—"Wait, are you telling that that you two, no it couldn't have been you."

Looking from one to the other, I knew, it was true. My friends, my buddies, beat up my boyfriend within an inch of his life. I felt the bile rising and thought I'd lose it right then.

"Wait, Henry said there were three guys."

"We got Sammy to come along too, in case we needed reinforcements," added Chris.

"Reinforcements?! You didn't think two of you with lead pipes ambushing an unarmed man in an alley was enough? My God, do you know how bad this is? I have to let that detective know. How could you be so stupid, so irresponsible, so, so, violent?"

I was shouting by this time. Furious doesn't come close to how angry I was. I could feel my face getting hotter and knew it was bright red and my eyes filled up. I was one hot mess but all I could think of was Henry lying there, broken and it was my 'friends' who did that to him.

"We was just tryin' ta help, Elliot."

"Well, you sure did a great job of it, Bud. You know Henry was almost dead when he was brought here. Do you know, do you have any conception of how badly he's injured? Let me enlighten you. He has a shattered optical bone and will need surgeries on that so he can see out of that eye again. He's got a collapsed lung from the broken ribs you gave him. His kneecap is fractured, and they are replacing it now, along with the ankle that's broken in two places. The doctor is also concerned with internal injuries."

"We just knew he was hurting you and we wanted him to hurt too."

"Well, Chris, you certainly accomplished that. Henry was already hurting from me screaming at him to get out. Didn't either of you see the look on his face when he got out of the car? He was devastated, as angry as I was, even I saw that."

"You really gonna turn us in?"

"I have to, I don't have a choice. I can't go back and sit with Robin acting like I don't know anything and it's just wrong and mean what you did."

"Then, we better get going. You can't blame us for getting a head start."

"Go ahead, you won't get very far. The detective on the case is a friend of Henry's as well. He's gonna be out for blood. So, go ahead, run boys. See how far you get. And don't forget to pick up Sammy on the way."

"C'mon, Bud. Let's get the fuck outta here."

"Right behind ya, man."

I watched them hurry out of the room and immediately fell into a chair. I was shaking so badly I thought I'd break a tooth. My stomach was churning and knew I had to get to the lavatory, quickly. I just made it into a stall and lost it. I cleaned up and started back to Robin, wondering the whole time how I was ever going to tell her, but I had to and then on to Detective Stone.

"Where have you been? The doctor came out a couple of minutes ago. Hunter's in recovery and doing fine. Doctor White said the operations went smoothly and they also got his lung inflated."

"Oh, Robin that's fantastic news." With tears welling up, I reached over and grabbed Robin and we hugged. I felt like a weight had been lifted, if not completely, at least partially. I felt so damn guilty about Chris, Bud, and Sammy, plus the fact that if I hadn't thrown Henry out, he wouldn't have been in that alleyway in the first place.

I looked down at Robin and she was smiling with tears streaming down her rosy cheeks. She really was a pretty girl if one took the time to really see her.

"I'm so relieved, you know I was feeling guilty about Hunter getting hurt."

"Why on earth would you feel that way? From what I've seen, you are there for him all the time. You're a true-blue friend, Robin."

"Because we usually go jogging together but I was busy with a story this morning and blew him off. Usually, I'd have made breakfast for us and he wouldn't have been in the alley at all."

"Now, Robin, you can't think like that. I'm the guilty one. I kicked him to the curb and left him alone and hurting. This is on me."

"Elliot, Hunter told me the whole story and I have to say I wasn't thrilled with his deception. He honestly thought it was the best way to get the story. After he met you and you guys got so, um, close, he felt bad about it all. He kept telling me that he was going to come clean with you and hoped you would forgive him. He was petrified that you would react just the way you did. Now, I'm not accusing you, I really don't blame you and if I'd been in your shoes, I would have done the same thing, if not worse."

"That's extremely generous of you to say. I can't help but feel responsible. I have something to tell you."

"Okay, shoot."

Elliot motioned behind him with his arm straight out, "Well, my, uhm friends that were here? They just told me—."

"There you are. Robin was getting pretty anxious that you weren't here for the news."

"Sorry, Doc, I was talking with a couple of friends of mine."

"I wanted to let you both know; Hunter is out of recovery and on his way to his room. Give the nurses a few minutes to get him settled and you can go in. He's in room eleven eleven in the Capron wing."

"Thanks Doc," Elliot said while shaking the doctor's hand profusely.

"Yes, thank you for saving Hunter's life."

"No need to thank me, it's my job. After you see him, I suggest you both take naps. The two of you look like hell!"

"You look like you could use some shut eye yourself, Doc."

"I can't argue with that, Elliot. It was a long, delicate situation. Hunter wasn't in any danger, but it took a lot of time to, well, put him back together. Now go on, both of you. If you walk slow enough, he should be ready to see you when you get there."

"All right, thanks again Doc. C'mon Elliot, let's go see our boy," Robin said as she linked arms with me.

"I'm with ya, let's go."

I was lighthearted at that moment, knowing Henry was going to be good as new. It would take time, of course, but he would be all right. Then I suddenly remembered Chris and Bud and I was back to being miserable. I still hadn't told Robin and I needed to talk to Detective Stone as soon as I possibly could. Robin seemed to sense my apprehension and unhooked my arm and took my hand. We walked hand in hand down the corridor to Henry's room. She had misinterpreted my mood, but it felt good to have somebody really care about me, especially after everything with Henry.

"Don't worry, Elliot. Hunter's going to be very happy to see you," Robin beamed. She reminded me of sunshine.

Walking into the room, all I saw at first were all of the tubes and wires going from various places around the hospital bed and disappearing under Henry's bedclothes. It made me shiver to think of what those guys had done to him and how we could be visiting him down in the morgue right now.

I stayed back and motioned to Robin with my head for her to approach him first. I watched him sleep and felt better knowing he was peaceful, at least for the moment.

"Hunter? Hunter, it's me, Robin. Time to wake up, sweetie. Can you hear me? Elliot, why don't you come over to the other side of the bed and see if he'll wake up for you."

I moved slowly and deliberately until I was up near his head. I bent down to his ear and whispered his name. Well, not really his name but the only one I'd known for a long time.

"Henry? It's Elliot. Robin's right, it's time to wake up. You're burning daylight, my friend."

"Mm, yeah, okay. Give me five more minutes," Hunter whispered.

"Okay, but only five, then you have to get up."

"Alright, Elliot. I will. Thanks for being here when I woke up; you too, Robin."

"Of course, sweetie. We wouldn't have been anywhere else, right Elliot?"

"Absolutely. Now, you get some rest and we'll be back to visit in a while."

"Sounds good, I'm just gonna rest my eyes a bit."

Rest his eyes, I had to laugh at that one, Henry was dead to the world in seconds.

"He'll sleep for hours. You two should get something to eat, then some sleep. I can call you when he starts to wake up if you'd like," offered Nurse Briggs.

"Yeah, Let's get out of here for a while and get some fresh air. Do you realize we've been in this hospital for almost fourteen hours?" Robin suggested.

"Yeah, we definitely need a break. Plus, I have a couple of errands to run. Why don't you go ahead, Robin. I'll be right behind if you don't mind."

"No of course not, take your time with him. I'll meet you outside.

I was compelled to speak to Henry, to make sure he heard my voice.

"Henry? Henry do you hear me?" I whispered. "I want you to know how horrified I was to have found out you had been beaten. I was so scared to think something this cruel could happen to you, to us. I want to get to know you, to laugh and cry with you. I want a chance to grow old with you, to tell you that I love you, Henry. I insist you make a full recovery. I'm leaving now, Robin is waiting, but I'll be back as soon as I can. Pleasant dreams, Henry," I said as I gave him a peck on the cheek and left to find Robin.

"When the nurse calls you, will you give me a call?" I asked Robin after finding her waiting for me in the lobby.

"Of course, I will," Robin replied as we walked out the main doors to the parking lot. The air smelled so good after breathing 'hospital air' for hours.

"Mm, smell that air, it's wonderful."

"Yeah it's clean and you can catch a hint of the flowers too. My car is over that way," I said while pointing.

"Okay, I'm in the opposite direction." Hugging, I felt closer to her and to Henry as well.

"I will call you as soon as she calls me. Be safe and see you later."

"Thanks, and you as well."

I got to my car and slid down into the seat. I had to get to the police station and talk to Detective Stone, immediately.

Chapter Seven
Finally Looking Up

Before I knew it, I was pulling up in front of the police station. I figured it was better to get there and get this over with. I parked and walked up to the reception area. There were a couple of people ahead of me, but the line moved swiftly.

"Can I help you?" asked a burly man with a deep, resounding voice.

"I need to speak with Detective Stone, please."

"Is he expecting you?"

"No, but you can tell him I have information regarding the beating in the alleyway behind the Kozy Kitchen."

"Your name?"

"Elliot Scott."

"The actor?"

"Yeah."

"Whad'ya know. My sixteen-year-old goes bonkers over you!"

"That's great to hear. Would you like an autographed picture? I always keep a few on me, just in case." Reaching into my inside jacket pocket, I pulled out an 8 x 10 glossy of my smiling face.

"What's her name?"

"Maureen. Thank you, this is extremely nice of you."

"No problem, man. Here you are. May I see Detective Stone now?"

"Let me buzz the office again."

"Have a seat on the bench, Mr. Scott. I'll see if I can round him up."

"Great."

It only took a minute for him to come out. "Hello, Elliot, come on back to my office."

I followed him through some of the dirtiest places I'd ever seen, and we were in the police station!

"Have a seat," he offered while pulling a chair out for me. I sat gingerly at the edge of the chair. "Now, what can I do for you? Hunter is okay, isn't he?"

"Yes, he's out of surgery and resting in his room. The doctor said he came through great and should make a full recovery. Of course, we still have to wait for *The Eye* specialist to determine the damage there."

"So far, it's great news all around. So, tell me, why do you look like ten miles of rough road?"

"Um, yeah. I, ah, I need to tell you something. This is not easy for me at all."

"Take your time and just let it out."

"I, um, I know who beat up Hen—Hunter."

"What?"

"Yeah, it was a couple of friends, or rather ex-friends of mine. They showed up at the hospital to see me and started bragging about it. We got into a huge fight, and I told them I was coming to you. They said they were going to take off, but knowing them, they only got as far as my place."

"Elliot, who are they and why would they have done this?"

"They did it because Hen—Hunter had lied to me and hurt me. They were trying to retaliate and get revenge. I told them we'd made up, or at least called a truce. Their names are Chris Young, Bud Vickers, and Sammy Gold was also there, according to Bud."

"All right thank you for coming in. I know it's not easy ratting out a friend. Let me get an APB out, I'll be right back."

I sat nervously bobbing my knee up and down. Did Stone believe me? Was he coming back with a cop to haul me to jail? I couldn't go to jail, I had to be there for Henry when he woke up.

"Okay, I've got police headed for your house now. You have to stay away from there until I give you the all clear, you got it?"

"Yes, sir. I wouldn't want to be there, especially if they try something stupid and end up getting shot. Together they make up almost a whole brain. I just never thought they were violent or would actually hurt anyone. It makes me sick every time I think about what they did. I feel totally responsible for it."

"No, Elliot, you can't blame yourself for someone else's actions. Did you tell them to go beat up Hunter?"

"Absolutely not, but I did go on and on how he'd hurt me and how could he have done that and how bad I felt, and I guess they transferred it to violence and revenge. That's why I feel so bloody guilty. Now, how am I going to face Henry and tell him it was my friends that did that to him. And Robin... she'll probably never forgive me, she's so protective of him, as she should be."

"I bet when you explain the whole story, neither of them will blame you. I'm going to the hospital to see how Hunter is doing, I'll also explain the situation and I'm sure it will be okay."

"Thanks, Detective, that's really great of you to do that. You and Henry, you're good friends then?"

"Actually, he called me with a research project, and I helped him out with it. I haven't known him long but feel as if I know him well."

"That's him. He has a way of becoming close in a very short period of time. Is it okay if I hang around here for a while? I'd like to know when those three idiots are brought in, Henry is sleeping, and I can't go home anyway."

"Sure, you stay as long as you need to. I've got work to do, here come over to this desk, it's empty today. There's coffee in the corner over there, it's a quarter a cup and there are vending machines around the corner in the next room."

Thanks, a cup of coffee sounds wonderful."

I fixed myself a cup and headed back to the desk assigned to me. It was in the back of the room, so I had a clear shot of the entire squad room. It was fascinating to watch the cops. There were only two or three left after Stone issued the order of going after 'my friends'. They were bantering back and forth and then they'd get quiet and whisper. I, of course, assumed they were discussing me and what happened.

My phone chirped, signaling a text. Checking, I saw it was from Robin.

'Got home and tried to sleep. Not easy. I'm tired but I can't shut my mind down. Thought I'd check on how you're doing. So how are you doing? I'm thinking if you're feeling like me, maybe we could meet up and get a bite somewhere. Let me know.'

'Hey, Robin, I know what you mean about sleeping. I would love to get a bite but I'm right in the middle of something. I'll explain when I see you. The moment I'm free, I'll text you. Thanks for checking on me.'

WAKING UP WAS A NIGHTMARE. I opened my eyes through a thickness of fog. I tried moving my arm and the pain jolted throughout my entire body. Looking around, seeing machines blinking and beeping, I concluded I was in the hospital, but what happened to me and how did I get here.

As I contemplated various scenarios, the doctor walked in.

"Hunter, you're awake. How are you feeling? If you're in any pain at all, tell me. The nurses have permission to give you whatever you need."

As he spoke, the entire episode flooded back into my memory. I remembered every whack with the lead pipes and how much each one hurt. I also remembered Robin and Elliot being there, was that real or wishful thinking?

"Your friends will be back in a while. They'd been here for hours, so I sent them home. Hunter, can you hear me?"

"Yeah, yeah, doc, I can. It's all rushing back to me. I remember everything. But I still can't see their faces."

"You took quite a beating. All and all, you were damn lucky to have survived this ordeal. Dr. Jewett, the ophthalmologist, should be here anytime to assess the damage and lay out a plan."

"You said he's one of the best, right?"

"Um, yes, but he's a she. Dr. Rachel Jewett is one of the best surgeons I have ever worked with. She doesn't just fix and stitch, she is a true artist, and she's a wonderful person."

"Jeez, Jerome, you make me sound like some kind of goddess."

Dr. White and I turned quickly and saw a beautiful lady standing in the doorway. She had long blonde hair and bright blue eyes that sparkled. She had the features of a porcelain doll and any fears I may have been harboring, dissipated.

"Rachel! I'm so glad you made it," Dr. White exclaimed as the two embraced, warmly.

"This is our patient, Hunter Wilson. He was beaten with several lead pipes. I have all of the X-rays here and full reports on his condition. He just returned from surgery about an hour ago to re-inflate his lung and reconstruct his kneecap along with setting his ankle. He's doing great, but now we need your expertise for his eye."

"Hello, Dr. Jewett. It's nice to meet you," I said while holding my hand out. She readily took it, and I felt a good strong and confident grip.

"Nice to meet you, too. Although I'm sorry it's under such dreadful circumstances."

"Rachel, while you do your exam, I'm going to grab a bite and Hunter, I'll call your friend Robin, if you'd like me to. I told her I would let her know when you woke up. She and that other friend of yours, Elliot wouldn't budge until you were out of the OR and resting comfortably in your room. You've got quite the cheerleading team there."

"Robin has been a good friend for a good many years. Elliot, is, well, a newer friend, but just as important. Yes, I would appreciate you calling them."

"It looks like you've been through the ringer. Looking at your X-rays, the left orbital bone has been shattered."

"Can you fix that?" I followed Dr. Jewett as she moved about the room. " It sounds bad and complicated."

"Complicated is my middle name. Seriously, I'll need to sit with all of this material and figure out the best way to begin. See, we have to be careful that your eyeball fits into any new socket that is created. Once I have a plan, you and I will sit down together, and I'll go over every inch of it with you."

"Thank you, I like that. I would like a couple of friends to join in on the discussion, if that's okay with you."

"Absolutely, this is your eye, you get to call the shots. Let me take all of this and get to work. I may be back in a while to take some measurements of the area around *The Eye*."

"You do whatever you need to, I'll be here," I said, smiling.

"That attitude will go a long way in speeding your full recovery. It's nice to see that."

"I've always been an optimist, doc. I must admit, I'm a little shaky about the whole thing, but I'm really trying to keep my spirits up and with doctors like you and Dr. White and the good friends I have, I really think I'm going to make a full recovery."

"Excellent, Hunter. I intend on making that a reality, but I will have a better idea after looking everything over. I do have a ninety four percent success rate when it comes to this surgery so there's that. I'll be back in a while; you get some rest."

"I will, and thanks again, Dr. Jewett."

I watched her, out of my one good eye, as she went out the door. I was feeling much more confident and hoped Robin and Elliot would be back soon.

Even though I knew it was the right thing to do, I felt guilty about turning Bud, Chris, and Sammy in. Robin had called to say Henry was awake. We decided to wait on getting a bite until after we saw him. I was thrilled to know he was up but walked around with the weight of the world on my shoulders, I blamed myself for the beating. If I hadn't acted like such a baby, throwing that giant-sized tantrum, the boys wouldn't have thought to retaliate, and Henry wouldn't be in the hospital.

"Excuse me, detective, have you heard anything?" I asked as I found Stone out at the front desk.

"I was just getting the report and coming down to you. The house was empty, but there are signs they had been there. Do you know where they might have gone?"

"Have you checked at their own places?"

"Yes, of course, but there are definite signs they were at your residence."

"They sometimes hang out at Griffith Park, but that's about all I know. They always hang out at my place. I was asking because I got a call from Robin. Henry is awake. I'd like to get to the hospital."

"Oh, that's great news, yes of course, go. I'll call you when I hear anything. I'll be joining the hunt now."

All kinds of thoughts whirled around in my mind while driving to the hospital. I was still nervous about Henry. He seemed fine with me, but what happens when he finds out who beat him up? I wish it were weeks from now and everything was settled, but no sense in thinking that way. I'm going to have to bite the bullet and tell Henry the truth, the whole truth and let the chips fall where they may. I worry about Robin too. She finds out the truth, she may never forgive me and that would be heartbreaking.

Pulling into the lot, I immediately saw Robin jumping out of her car and was able to park next to her.

"Hello, stranger," Robin called with a wave.

"Hey, long time no see," I replied.

We both laughed and walking hand in hand, headed off to see our common denominator.

Chapter Eight

The Whole Story, Interrupted

"KNOCK KNOCK," ROBIN said as they sauntered through the doorway of my room.

"Knock knock yourselves, come on in!" I couldn't help but smile. " I've been wondering when you'd get here. Dr. White said he called you a while ago."

"I know, but we both had some errands to run, and I needed a shower and a change of clothes," Robin explained.

"Same here, Henry. We got here as fast as we could. I know it's hard for you, having to lie here and wait for everything. It's not easy for a take charge guy like you, but you're going to have to get used to it, at least for a while."

"Yeah, you're right, I am feeling cooped up, but if I try to even change positions, I'm quickly reminded why I'm here in the first place."

"Has *The Eye* specialist come yet?" Robin asked.

"Yes, and I like her very much. Her name is Jewett, Dr. Rachel Jewett. She is going to have a consultation on the best course to take with my eye and she wants me to be included, and also you two are invited as well."

"Us? Really?"

"Yeah, Elliot. She said it was my eye and I should be in on all of the decision making. I asked if you two could join in as well, and she said absolutely."

"Wow, she does sound special, thanks for asking about us, Hunter," Robin added.

"We are in this together, right? Kinda like the Three Musketeers," I laughed.

I noticed Elliot got a funny look on his face when I said that, like he'd just eaten a sour pickle. I also realized he was keeping a fair amount of distance between us. Robin was right up by my head, but Elliot was practically standing in the doorway.

"Elliot, is something wrong? Did something happen after you left earlier?" I asked.

"Um, yeah, I, ah, got something to tell you. You and Robin. Ya see –"

"Hello everyone. I need to get a fresh set of vitals on our boy. Would you all mind stepping out for just a minute or two? Great, thanks," Nurse Briggs said as she guided Robin and Elliot out of the room without waiting for an answer.

"Nurse Briggs, do you know when Dr. White or Dr. Jewett might be back? I'm anxious to get started."

"They were still in a conference room going over papers, charts, diagrams and X-rays just now as I passed by. It shouldn't be too much longer."

"Thanks."

"No problem. Your vitals look good. You're making an incredible recovery. It's only been a few hours since surgery, but you're awake and orientated. Vitals are strong, too. I have no doubt you'll come through *The Eye* surgery just fine. Of course, I'm not really supposed to say that" Nurse Briggs winked at me as she commented.

"It's alright, I won't tell anyone. I appreciate the positive attitude."

"We do, too. It really does help with getting better much faster and it makes for a happier, healthier patient. All set, I'll send your friends back in."

"See you soon, I'm sure," I teased.

Nurse Briggs was one of the nicest people I've ever met. She reminds me of Robin.

"Hey, the nurse said you were doing very well, and we could come back."

"Yup, on the mend. Where's Elliot?"

"Men's room."

"Does he seem a little off to you?"

"Off, like what?"

"Like staying across the room, not even close enough to me to touch or hold hands. He also looks guilty about something. I don't know, Robin. There's something hiding behind his eyes."

"He has been rather quiet, ever since we left earlier. He had stuff to do so I went home, and he went off to do his thing and he did say he needed to tell us something just before the nurse came in."

"Yeah, okay, we'll ask him when he gets back in here."

No sooner were the words out of my mouth when he walked into the room.

"Elliot, you said you had something to tell Robin and me. No time like the present."

"You're right, I'm trying to build up the courage to tell you."

"Spit it out quickly, like taking a band aid off," Robin offered.

"I, ah, I know who did this to you, Henry," Elliot whispered.

"Who?" Robin asked.

"How do you know?" I added.

"Because it was done for me," Elliot said with his head down.

"For yo- wait, did Bud and Chris have anything to do with it?"

"Yeah, Henry, they did."

"I don't understand," Robin said.

"I do. They beat me up in retaliation for what I did to Elliot. Is that right?"

"Yes, that's exactly what happened. I've tried to make it right. Robin, I was at the police station this afternoon when you called me. I went to see Detective Stone and told him the whole story. He's got an APB out on the three of them. No doubt he will flush them all out soon."

"Who was the third one?"

"It was Sammy. He only went along for the promise of beer. Chris and Bud won't tolerate him much longer."

I was stunned, in shock really. I knew these guys, not well, but I'd talked and drank with all of them over at Elliot's. I could tell he hadn't had anything to do with it, nobody could fake a look like he had. His face kept changing from a sickly green to ashen. I did have a couple of questions though.

"How did you find out they were the ones that attacked me?"

"I know how," Robin interjected. "They showed up here, and you went off with them to that conference room. When you came back, you were different. You'd become very quiet, uncomfortable. You'd barely look at me. I thought it was worry over Hunter, but."

Elliot had moved up closer to me and put his hands on the bed guard. I took full advantage of that and placed my hand over his. He just stood there, staring at me. His eyes glistening with unshed tears and such a sad face.

"Elliot, this is not your fault. I understand the guilt, I know I would've reacted the same way, but I honestly don't blame you one iota. Also, I get why the guys did it. They're loyal to you, you were hurtin', so they hurt back. Not that I want them to get off scott-free, mind you, but I don't think they should be thrown in jail, either."

"No, Henry, they do. They bragged so much about the whole thing, even when I told them how wrong it was and how they needed to turn themselves in, they were so cocky about the incident. They didn't bring

Sammy down here, but like I said, they won't put up with him for long. He'll be whining, wanting to go home. It makes me sick, they actually thought I was going to praise them for what they'd done. I can't believe that you and Robin haven't tossed me out the door on my ass."

"This isn't your fault. You were hurt over Hunter, that couldn't be helped and perfectly understandable. These friends of yours were trying to protect you and get revenge for you, I understand that as well. They just went way too far. But Hunt and I," Robin gestured, " we aren't going to take it out on you. That'd be like shooting the messenger, right?"

"Robin's right. This all stems from my deception, so you could say, I can only blame myself for this predicament."

"I'm very grateful to both of you. Detective Stone said he would be in touch as soon as he knew anything, but he'd gotten practically the entire police force out looking for them. I want them punished for what they did, but not killed."

"I agree. Hopefully Joe will have news soon," I said as a wave of yawns attacked my mouth.

"You're sleepy. Why don't you get some rest," Robin wrinkled up her cute nose. " I need to get down to the office for a bit and work on a story. Do you want me to tell Woolridge about you?"

"Yeah, go ahead, not that he'll give a shit. Just don't let him bully you, Robin. Knowing him, he'll want you to cover the story."

"Oh, don't worry. I've been handling him for years. I'll be back later on," Robin said as she bent to kiss my forehead. Then she gave Elliot a huge hug and a kiss on the cheek.

"See ya later, fellas."

"Bye Robin."

"See ya, Robin."

Elliot slid a chair over to the side of the bed on my right side so I could see him. He bent down and gave me a passionate kiss and then sat in the chair, still holding my hand.

"I can't tell you how sorry I am for everything. We wouldn't be here if I'd only left well enough alone. I had to chase the story with no regard for you and your privacy. I thought it would make me a big shot with my boss. Huh, he couldn't give a shit about me. When I told him, you'd found out the truth and there was no story, he up and fired me. Gave me ten minutes to pack my stuff and get out. Man, I'd worked my butt off for him for over five years, and just like that I'm out the door."

"I can't help but feel responsible for that, but truthfully, I'm glad no stories of me went into that rag, or any form of media. I don't like my life spread out for anyone to read about. Besides, there's really nothing to tell."

"Oh, I beg to differ, Elliot. There are plenty of skeletons in your closet to be explored, but not for the media, for you to know where you come from."

"What do you mean? You actually found something from my past? You were gonna put it in that rag you work for?"

"I don't work for that rag anymore. Remember, I was fired? I also just said I wasn't giving anything to the media, I just think you have a right to know about your past, your childhood."

"I think I know enough about it, thank you," Elliot snapped.

"I'm not trying to upset you, Elliot. You have a right to know about your biological parents. I can give that to you."

"Wait, my biological parents? What do you know about them? I was told the files were sealed and I couldn't find out anything. The couple that I thought were my parents, Jerry and Kiki Scott, they told me my parents had died and that's how they adopted me. Now you say there's a story?"

"Yes, I've seen it with my own eyes. I have a box of materials at my place that will prove what I'm telling you. I've been working with Detective Stone; his father worked your parents case."

"Case? My parents had a case? Are you sure you're not thinking of my adoptive parents? They drank and treated me like I was non-existent and partied all night, every night. When they drank, they got mean and they drank almost every night. The not so famous Jerry and Kiki Scott. I was embarrassed and ashamed of them growing up. Then when I was fourteen, they announced that I wasn't really their son. They had unselfishly taken me in from a fate worse than death, first as a foster child, and then adoption. Finding this out, I felt free, for the first time in my life but I had plenty of questions. Who were my real parents? Were they still alive? Why did they give me up? Neither Jerry nor Kiki would talk about them, not even after getting stinkin' drunk. The two of them packed their stuff one day and said they were moving to New York to try their hand at Broadway. They left a ton of shit in one of my spare closets, gave me a lecture about how I wouldn't be the star I was if it hadn't been for them, and promptly left. That was over a year ago and I haven't regretted them leaving a single minute. Now is probably a great time to throw all those boxes of crap out, since I'm cleaning house, so to speak. Hell, I might just sell the whole house. Getting fired from a blockbuster movie is not the way to maintain star status. I may be a nobody in a few days. I could use the money from the sale to get a modest house way out somewhere, maybe Topanga Canyon."

"Jeez, I'm sorry they treated you like that. I love the way you are so resilient and able to bounce back from all the tragedy in your short life."

"You're back to talking about the parents that threw my away, right?"

"Not exactly threw away, but let's just say your parents had some issues to work out and they wanted to protect you."

"Protect me? From what? C'mon Henry, give me somethin' here."

"You were born John Thomas Benson. Your parents, Thomas and Mary Benson, called you Johnny. They, ah, died, when you were four years old, and you were put into the foster system."

"They both died? As in together? Was it a car accident?"

"Yes, they died together, but it wasn't an accident, exactly. Your parents were –"

"Hunter my boy! I just got the word you were here. You should've called me, son."

"Jeez, you scared me. Elliot, this is my former boss, Stanley Woolridge. Woolridge, this is Elliot Scott."

"Oh, you're the one with the secret, sordid past that Wilson won't reveal. Ya know, if you tell me your tale, I can get you top dollar, but only for a limited time. The way I hear it, you're on your way out the door. Getting yourself canned from a Hovis production? Not too bright, kid."

"Woolridge cut the crap. He's not telling you shit and big fuckin' deal, it's one picture. With Elliot's talent, he'll be flooded with offers."

"You're the one that fired Hunter? Considering he's the best reporter you got down there, it was rather a foolish thing to do, don't you think? Now, from Hunter's point of view, it's perfect. He can apply to reputable newspapers and magazines and get a real job."

I laid there in my hospital bed, barely able to move and listened to the man I was falling for defend me, even though he wasn't totally convinced of my honesty. My heart was bursting with emotion, with, love. I couldn't help the feeling, and I was pretty sure it was written all over my face. Elliot glanced at me and did a double take. He stood there with a small, shy smile on his face, and I watched him turn pink. It slowly rose from his neck to his prominent cheekbones and onto his ears. I couldn't help but smile, it was the cutest thing I'd ever seen. Woolridge just stood there looking at us and shaking his head.

"You two deserve each other, good day gentlemen," Woolridge sputtered as he jammed his bowler onto his too big head.

"Yes, we do, don't we!" Elliot called after him. "Wow, what a dickhead," Elliot stated, shaking his head.

"Yeah, and he was actually nice today, for him that is."

"Now, back to my parents. You were saying –,"

"Hey you two, I'm baaaack!" Robin announced.

"Hi, Robin."

"Hello, Robin," Elliot said quietly.

"Did I, uh, interrupt something? I can leave if -,"

"No, of course not. Henry and I were just talking about your boss. You just missed him."

"Woolridge was here?"

"Yeah, hat in hand too. I think he was trying to get the story out of me."

"I believe it. He's scuzzy enough to try," Robin agreed. "Any news from the specialist?"

"No, not yet. I suppose she needs to be thorough, after all, it's my eye we're talking about."

"Did something happen, Robin? You were going to be gone a good long while," I asked.

"No, I forgot my small bag here," Robin explained while reaching under the bed. She pulled out a canvas bag, small in dimensions, huge in significance to her. This was determined by the way her whole face brightened.

I was getting antsy lying-in bed, without a way out. I think that's what was getting to me, I wouldn't be able to get out of there if some disaster did occur. My breathing started to become uneven. My heart was beating faster and the more I tried to slow it down, the more it sped up. I could feel beads of sweat popping out all over my face and I could only make tiny little sounds. I kept trying to signal to my visitors until finally Elliot looked up at me.

"Oh my God, Henry!" Elliot yelled as he rushed to my side.

"Hunt? What's going on with you," Robin said as she put her hand on my forehead.

"He's having trouble breathing I pushed the button for the nurse."

"Good, Elliot. We have to remain calm here. I'll run out to the nurses' station." Robin offered.

I could hear her running down the hall in her silly heels while Elliot was rubbing my back and had put a cool cloth on my forehead.

"Shh shh. Try to stay calm, take slow, even breaths."

"What's going on here?" Dr. White demanded.

"Cccan't bbbreeeeettthe." I wheezed.

"It came on suddenly, Doc. We were talking and Bam!" Elliot conveyed.

"All right, Hunter. I know it's difficult but try to slow down your breathing. Slowly breath in, then out."

"Doctor, I have the injection," Nurse Briggs said as she walked into the room.

"Thanks, let me have it and get me a small paper bag, please."

"Here you are." Briggs said.

"I have a paper bag right here," Robin announced.

"Good, bring it to me."

I was starting to really panic now, but then the doctor injected the needle into my IV and then placed the paper bag over my face.

"Here you go, Hunter. Breathe in and out through the bag. Slow it down, take deep breaths. You're going to be fine. You're hyperventilating. You're breathing so fast, you're getting too much oxygen and that's making you lightheaded and I bet your extremities are tingling, aren't they?"

Doc was right about all of it. I simply nodded.

"I get it, the paper bag gets him to breathe in carbon monoxide to counteract the overdose of oxygen, right?" Elliot asked.

"Right on the nose, plus I gave him a mild sedative to calm him down quicker. How are you doing, Hunter? Better now?" Doctor White asked as he took the bag away from my face.

"Yeah, I feel a lot better, thanks. I don't know what happened. I could feel the panic rapidly flowing up my body and then I couldn't breathe, couldn't talk. I felt myself sweating too. I tried to get your attention but neither of you were looking at me and that just added to my anxiety. Doc, was this a full-blown panic attack? If so, I don't ever want another one."

"Yes, it was a panic attack, but I'd say a rather mild one."

"Mild? Jeez, can you give me something so that doesn't happen again."

"I can do that, let me look up which one and the dosage level. I'll be back. We might also want to talk about therapists. I'm thinking you had a panic attack that was caused by PTSD. You rest now, that sedative should be kicking in soon and we'll talk more about this later."

"PTSD? You mean you think I have post-traumatic stress disorder? From the beating?"

"Yes, I do. But let's discuss it after you've rested. Elliot, Robin, stay a few more minutes then I 'd like Hunter to have absolute silence. You can come back tomorrow, sound fair?"

"Yeah doc. After what just happened, I want him to be as comfortable as possible," Elliot replied.

"Me too, doc, absolutely," Robin added.

I was barely conscience when the room emptied out. I drifted off dreaming of how lucky I was. I had a reason for tomorrow.

Chapter Nine

Elliot Knows Everything Now

I SLEPT, ACTUALLY SLEPT through the night. I woke to a brilliant blue, cloudless sky. This is extremely rare in L.A. I checked my phone, no messages. Another good omen where Henry was concerned. I dialed the hospital to find out how his night had been, and a very business-like nurse named Ms. Ryle explained Hunter had had a restful night and she and her nursing staff were quite busy taking care of the patients. She said if I wanted to know his condition, I should come see for myself. I thanked her and hung up. Not even her miserable attitude could alter my positive mood. I would get down there, right after a shower and some breakfast.

My phone buzzed and I answered it. "Hello?"

"Hi, Elliot, it's Joe Stone."

"Yes detective. You have news?"

"Yes, we apprehended the three suspects an hour ago. They're all here in lockup waiting for arrangement."

I couldn't speak, I felt relief, guilt, sadness, and rage all rolled into one package.

"Elliot? You there? Did you hear me?"

"Yeah, sorry, detective. I was just debating if I should come down there, to see what happens to them. Do you think they'll make bail?"

"I doubt it. The severity of the crime, plus their trying to get out of town, I don't see any judge being lenient with those three. I would go down quickly if you wanted to be there. Very few cases on the docket this morning. The judge will get to them in no time."

"Are you going?"

"Yes, but I'm the arresting officer, I can call you and let you know the outcome. "

"I think you're right. I really need to distance myself from them. Yeah, if you could let me know how it goes, I'd appreciate it. Talk with you later, bye."

"So long, Elliot."

Hey, Henry, I'm back! Turning the corner into his room, I saw at once Henry was not happy at all.

"Hi, what's wrong, babe?"

"Oh, hi, Elliot. I just got a call from Joe. He says the guys that beat me up have been arrested and are down at the police station awaiting their arraignment."

"Yeah, he called me as well. I decided to come see you, rather than go sit in the courtroom. I honestly don't want to see them again, it's a constant reminder of what I've done to you."

"You didn't do anything to me. Even though they picked the wrong execution, I do understand they were trying to protect you, an eye for an eye as it were."

"No, it's wrong, pure and simple. A violent assault on a fellow human being is never the right thing to do, not in my book. And speaking of my book, we are alone, would you please tell me about my parents?"

"Yeah, okay. Robin called and I asked her to go to my place and get the box of information. It's up to you if you want her to stay or go. She'll be here any minute."

"I'd honestly like to hear all of this in private if you don't mind. I've built it up so big in my mind, I'm really petrified about the truth. I don't mind Robin knowing, just not yet, if that's okay?"

"It's fine with me, Elliot," Robin said behind my back.

"Jeez, you scared me, girl! Good to see you. Did you hear, the three idiots that beat up Henry are in custody."

"Hooray! And I am sorry, Elliot. I know they're good friends of yours."

"They were friends of mine. I'm still in shock they'd go to such extremes."

"Here is the shoe box, Hunter," Robin said as she bent to kiss Henry. I'm going to head to the office. I've got to track down a lead for a new story. I'll stop by later on. Good luck, boys."

"Thanks, Robin. Come back and we can have lunch together."

"That would be nice, yes I'll do that. Elliot, I hope you can stay too. I'm off now, see you guys later."

I waited until she'd gone out the door then I walked over to Henry and kissed the stuffing out of him. I felt him responding as he wrapped his arms around my neck. We pulled away in sync, looked at each other and started to laugh.

"What's so funny?" Henry asked.

"I don't know, but you're laughing too," I replied.

"That was some kiss, wow. A few more like that and I'll make a full recovery in no time."

"I wanted you to know how much I care about you, Henry. I, ah, I'm falling in love with you. No matter what you tell me about my parents, I promise not to take it out on you."

"I'm falling in love with you, too, Elliot. I promise what I'm about to tell you will go no further than us. Robin can know, only if you say it's alright to tell her. This is nobody's business but yours and I'm sorry I snooped around and found out about it all. Joe Stone knows about the case, as it was his father that was in charge of the investigation. Sit down, babe. This is going to take a while."

I sat on the bed facing Henry as he opened the box and began to take yellowed newspaper articles out.

"As I told you yesterday, your biological parents were Thomas and Mary Benson. They were married April eighteenth, 1992. They had a child, a son named John Thomas Benson, born January 23, 1993, almost exactly nine months after they were married. Here, it's in this article here," Henry said as he handed me the age-worn rectangle. Taking the delicate piece of recorded history, I realized I was staring into the one-dimensional, black and white representation of the faces belonging to my parents.

"This is incredible, you sure these are my biological parents?"

"Yeah, we've collected enough evidence to be fairly certain. Of course, a DNA test would make it conclusive. Now brace yourself, Elliot. Here comes the really bad news."

"Bad news? You mean cuz they died? I'm coming to terms with that."

"No, the bad news is what your parents did for fun. You see this girl?" Henry asked as he handed me a picture of a young woman, early twenties, blonde and blue-eyed.

"Yeah, she's pretty, who is she?"

"She's Thom and Mary Benson's first kill. This is –"

"Wait, what did you just say? Their first what?"

"I'm sorry, Elliot. It's true, your parents were psychopaths who raped, mutilated, and killed twenty-seven people, of both genders, from February 14, 1993, until the end of their reign, August 13, 1997. They were gunned down, Bonnie and Clyde style, right in front of the Hollywood sign."

With a calmness that belied my horror of the entire situation, I took the photograph from Henry's trembling hand. I looked into his eyes and saw sadness and pain. I could tell this was killing him to tell me these outrageous truths about my flesh and blood. As he let go of the eight by ten, he took my hand and gave it a slight squeeze; I reciprocated.

Looking at the beautiful young lady in the photograph, I asked," Who was she?"

"She was Tina Driscoll. She was twenty years old and found in a dumpster. She had blue eyes and blonde hair. She was brutally murdered on February 14, 1993. From what Joe and I could determine, Tina was the first victim."

"How many did you say they had killed?"

"It was established by Detective Amos Stone, Joe's father, there were twenty-seven."

"And who killed them? My parents, I mean."

"Joe's dad and his team, Amos Stone. Then little Johnny was placed into foster care."

"Is that when I was taken by the Scotts?"

"No, first you were taken by a family named Sweeney, Owen and Natalie. They had four foster kids: Jack, Toby, Sarah and Millie. Jack's teacher suspected abuse as she had seen multiple bruises on him. The school checked all of them and found they'd all been abused. All of the children, including you, were taken away from them and the Sweeney's ended up in jail. That's when the Scotts took you in. I didn't know anything about the drinking, there was nothing about any of that in the reports."

"I, I don't know what to make of any of this. I'm overwhelmed. May I take all the information and look through it alone? I need time to sort it all out."

"Absolutely, Elliot. I get it, really. I was pretty blown away when I read all of it, and I'm not the one it's about."

"Thanks, and, um, thanks for not making any of this public. I can barely focus; I can't imagine it all in print."

"Yeah, I get it. Here take the whole box, bring it home and quietly read it all. Some of the photos are hard to take, I'm right here if you need anything. Call me or come back here and we can talk."

I looked at Henry and knew he was nothing but sincere. I saddled up close to him and gently slipped my arms around his neck. I gave him a kiss on the lips and laid my head on his shoulder. I felt so protected when he arms wrapped around me and he laid his chin on the top of my head.

"I'm gonna go so you can get your rest. Has Dr. Jewett been back in to see you?"

"She's been in to ask questions and take more x-rays and measurements. She said she'd have a definitive answer tomorrow morning."

"I'll be in to see you as soon as I can in the morning. I'm gonna be up probably all night. It will take time to go through all of this information and try to process it all. My head is still in a tizzy, and I need time by myself to sort through my feelings and to find out if I actually remember any of this."

"Yes, I'm sure you will, just call me if you start having bad thoughts, promise?"

"Yeah, I promise, Henry." I gave him another kiss, picked up the box and headed out with one more glance at that beautiful man lying in bed. He was already starting to drift off, so I quietly left the room and went home with a light heart and heavy shoulders.

Arriving home, I pulled the car into the garage, entered the house and shut the world out. I went into my father's study and thought how I'd turned it into a shrine all in hopes I'd feel less guilty with how I'd felt about him growing up. I was so embarrassed by both Jerry and Kiki. But after hearing about my biological parents, my adoptive set were practically up for fuckin' sainthood.

I spent half the night up with all of the gruesome pictures and the accounts of the horrific, unspeakable things that my parents did. I was only four years old, but the more I read, the more convinced I became that somewhere in my subconscious were memories from that period in my life, not the monstrous deeds of my own flesh and blood, but a memory somewhere rattling around.

I had fallen asleep before Elliot left with the box, but night terrors, bad dreams, things that go bump in the night, woke me up. Glancing at the clock on the wall, I knew I'd only been asleep a little over two hours. I hope that Elliot is getting some sleep and doesn't stay up all night with those articles and photographs consuming him.

While lying here cogitating, Nurse Beetle came in to take my vitals. "Mr. Wilson, what are you doing up?"

"I just woke up a minute ago. Do you ever get the feeling something bad's gonna happen?"

"I know what's gonna happen to you if you don't get to sleep soon," the nurse teased.

"I'm serious, has it? Ever happened to you?"

"Yes, as a matter of fact it did. About a month ago, I woke up in a cold sweat with a feeling of impending doom."

"Yeah, that's what I'm talking about," I said, excitedly. "What happened?"

"Nothing at first, but I couldn't shake that feeling so I called the hospital and found out one of my patients had died."

"That's what I'm talking about."

"Yes, but this patient was very old and very sick. He wasn't expected to make it through the night."

"But you still had a strong reaction to his death and that's what I'm talkin' about."

"Yes, that's true. You think you had a premonition?"

"I don't know, I just feel that something is going to happen, and it's not gonna be pretty," realizing I was rambling and not making much sense, I said, " Ah, don't listen to me, I'm probably paranoid, not being able to get up and walk around. I always wear off extra energy by pacing the room, I miss it."

"You're making great strides towards a complete recovery. Dr. White said he's never seen anyone heal as fast as you. We just have to concentrate on that eye of yours."

"Dr. Jewett said after she studies the file and the x-rays, she'll come see me with a plan."

"Yes, and she is one of the best in the country, all the doctors say it."

"Glad to *yawn* hear it. Oh, excuse me."

"Sounds like somebody is ready to sleep. Scooch down and let me cover you over," Nurse Beetle draped the soft, warm blanket over me. " There now you go to sleep. I'm going to go check on some other patients now."

I felt better, but I went back to sleep with the distinct feeling something bad was going to happen. I hoped it was me this black thing happened to, that way I'd know my friends were all safe. I was really tired now; I went back to sleep, dreaming of seeing Elliot in the morning.

Chapter Ten
Here We Go Again

It was another bright blue-sky day. Sun streaming down, making the morning fresh, crisp, and clean. I called the hospital and was told Henry had slept pretty well after midnight and was feeling alert and very little pain. I informed the nurse I would be there in a half hour or so. I tried calling Robin, but she wasn't picking up. I figured she was chasing some lead and I'd hear from her later. I decided to stop at the bakery two blocks from the hospital and bring coffee and a treat to Henry.

Walking in, several people turned to stare and quickly look away. Over the years, I'd gotten used to that. I'm recognized and people want to talk to me, stare at me, point in my face or ask for an autograph. Sometimes, they want all of them. This morning, however, they were acting oddly. No one was smiling, in fact, they all looked pretty pissed. I gave my order to the lady behind the counter, and she told me to have a seat and she'd bring my order to me.

I didn't really feel like sitting, not the way everyone was staring, so I paced in the front of the store. On one of my loops around, I noticed a magazine rack and thought to bring Henry the morning paper. Life as I knew it, ended, three feet from that rack. There it was. Now I understood the stares and the odd looks. Blood was rushing through my veins and pounded in my head. It was like a train wreck. It was horrible, yet one couldn't turn away. That's what it was like for me as I continued to stare at that rag called *The Eye*. The headline read, Superstar Elliot Scott. Raised by psychopaths with 27 rapes, mutilations and murders. See inside for the whole story.

"Oh, Mr. Scott. I was trying to keep you from seeing that. I asked, but Mr. Jenkins wouldn't let me take them down."

"It's okay, Penny. I would like to buy one, how much?"

"No, you take one, no charge. It's the least I can do. Here's your coffee and treats."

"Thank you." I grabbed the boxes and tucked the paper under my arm. I flew out the door and fell back against the building while taking in gulps of fresh air. I stood up straight and headed to my car. I had one purpose and one mantra repeating in my brain. "No, it can't be true."

At the hospital, I whipped my car into the first spot I encountered and ran up the hill to the main entrance. I didn't bother with the elevator; it was too slow, and I had too much nervous energy. I made it to Henry's room and stopped dead. I refused to believe he had done this to me, but who else even knew all of this? I was scared he would admit it and make me the fool, or he would deny it and I find out he was lying. I felt sick, but I had to know the truth. I barged into his room and marched right up to his bed.

"Hey, Elliot. I'm glad you're here, I – Elliot? What's wrong? Did something happen?"

"Happen? Well, you could say that. What can you tell me about this?" I said as I threw the paper in his face.

"What's th-" Henry said as he picked the paper up and read it.

I watched his face very carefully go from pink to bright red to a sickly green and finally deathly white. He looked up at me and there was excruciating pain in his eye, more so than when he'd been beaten to a pulp, but just because he was remorseful, doesn't mean he didn't run the story.

"You got an explanation for this, Henry?"

Slowly, he looked up from the paper in his hands, and shook his head. "I did not put this in the paper. I never gave the story to my editor, I never even typed it, there is no written copy of this anywhere, I swear Elliot. Wait a sec," Henry said as he grabbed the paper again. "Look at the byline, it reads Anonymous. You know if I'd done it, I would have used my own name."

"Maybe you didn't cuz you intended to use this rouse to make me think just that, when all along you intended to publish your precious article."

"You think I set this all up? What? getting Robin to go along, my boss to come down here just when you were here, do you think I paid your friends, your friends, mind you, to beat me up? Or maybe that's fake too. Maybe there's nothing wrong with me and it's all makeup!" Henry shouted at me. He was shaking and his machines were having apoplexy with all of their beeping. I ran out to the corridor and saw Nurse Briggs.

"Henry's upset and all the machines are going crazy."

"Let's go see what's going on," Briggs replied. We ran back into the room and Henry was breathing loud and hard and you could tell he was trying to slow it down. The machines had stopped beeping quite so much as well.

"That's it, Hunter. Slow and easy. Take your time. I'm going to give you something to relax you, nothing more, okay?"

I watched as he nodded his consent, and Nurse Briggs injected the medication into his IV. She'd also put an oxygen mask over his face and told him to use it for a couple of minutes until he was completely calm.

I was a mess. I was completely torn between believing him and thinking he'd been using me the whole time. I had to leave, if I stayed there any longer, I'd end up screaming at him, maybe take a poke at him myself. I had to sort this all out.

"Henry, I've got to get out of here. I need to think and can't do that in here with you. I want to believe you but there have been so many lies since I met you, I just don't know," I said as I hurried out of his room, down the corridor and out the front doors to freedom, but was I really free?

I watched my life run out of my room and I was devastated. I couldn't believe this was happening. I was calming down between the shot and the oxygen, but I was still shaking with anger. Who the fuck did this? Woolridge didn't have the story; I know it wasn't him. Robin didn't know the story either, plus, she was Robin, my very best friend. She'd never betray me. Joe knew most of the story, but what would he gain by selling it to *The Eye*? No, makes no sense it'd be him.

Maybe the article will give me a clue as to who wrote it. I felt sick about it, but it seems the only way to know. I began reading and had a touch of déjà vu. The more I read, the more familiar it sounded. Then, it hit me like a pile of bricks. This article was how I told the story to Elliot, verbatim. That means, oh no!

I began pushing the nurses call button erratically. The door opened promptly, and Nurse Beetle poked her head in.

"Yes, Hunter, what can I do for you?"

"I need to get in touch with my friend, Robin right away."

"You can give her a call but it's awfully early. She's probably sleeping."

"Knowing Robin, she's up, read the paper, getting in the shower and planning her day down to the last detail."

"Here's your phone, I'll give you some privacy," Nurse Beetle said as she picked up the instrument and handed it to me.

Dialing her number carefully, I listened to the tinny, mechanical ring. Thoroughly disappointed, I was about to hang up when I heard a click and a breathless Robin panted, "Hello?"

"Hey, Robin, it's Hunter. You okay?"

"Yeah, I was out getting coffee. Why are you calling me so early, what's going on, Hunt?"

"I'd rather not say over the phone, I think they're bugged ."

"Are you sure? And why would anyone do that?"

"Look, can you just get down here, I really need to talk to you about something," I was barely able to keep it together.

"Sure, yeah, just let me throw something decent on, and I'll come right over."

"Thank you, Robin, thank you ever so much."

Robin must have broken every speed limit because she arrived not ten minutes after I called her.

"Okay, Hunter, I'm here, what's the emergency and what's this about bugging the phones?"

I held up the copy of *The Eye* Elliot had so graciously left for me. Robin snatched it from my hands and read with open mouth, her eyes becoming wider as she read on and her breathing becoming a bit erratic.

"Robin, you alright?"

She looked up at me with her face reddened and contorted in pain. "Oh, Hunter. This is Elliot's secret? But who leaked it to the paper? I know you didn't, and I didn't know what the secret was, and no one else did either, so how did this happen?"

"I don't know but I intend on getting to the bottom of it if you'll help me. Elliot wants to believe me, but with everything that's happened, he's skeptical.

I felt such the coward running out on Henry like I did. I just couldn't stay in that room anymore. I continued to be of two minds, either wishing I'd never met Henry in the first place and not known anything about my "real" parents to wishing we'd already gone through it all and we'd emerged stronger than ever on the other side. I was also still reeling from this story going public. The intensity of outrage towards me personally was staggering. I was a child, a baby, when all of this went down. How can the general public blame me for it? How could anyone, after reading of the heinous crimes, think I had something, anything to do with it. Especially since I was a little boy. Do people actually think I'm a serial killer too?

Oh my God, that's exactly what the public thinks! That's why all of those people reacted the way they did at the bakery, they all think I'm a rotten apple, they probably want my head on a platter for what my parents did. I need to find out how Henry is doing, I thought as a picked up my cell and dialed the now familiar number.

"Hello, Elliot. How are you doing?"

"Pretty well, Robin. I wanted to know how Henry was doing. I know he was having surgery today."

"They took him almost three hours ago. The doctor said it would be long and tedious, but not to be worried that something went wrong, it's just so involved it's going to take a very long time. Of course, it's hard not to be concerned."

"Yeah, I know. I've been watching the time and contemplating when to call you."

"Do you want to come down here and keep me company?"

"I'm not sure, Robin. It's not you, I, I just don't know if I can handle that yet."

How about we meet somewhere else? We could go to the coffeeshop around the corner."

"Um, yeah, yeah okay. I'll do that. Give me ten minutes?"

"Absolutely, see you in a few."

It was really good to hear Robin's voice, I had to admit that to myself. I'm glad I let her talk me into meeting her. After all, it's just a cup of coffee."

I saw her head bobbing around, trying to see the door. The place was really crowded, and Robin was seated in the middle of the diner. I motioned towards her as a hostess ran over to seat me. She hurried me over and I quickly slid into the booth. Robin immediately took my hands and grinned, ear to ear.

"Robin, you have such a way of making a person feel wanted, important, and special all at once. Thank you for that."

"I really am this happy to see you, Elliot. I've missed you these last days, especially with Hunter going into surgery. I've missed having you to talk to and lean on."

"I've missed you too, but I think you have it backwards, I'm the one that does most of the leaning."

"Why don't we split the difference and call it a draw?"

"Sounds wonderful. That's you, Robin. Always the diplomat. So how has Henry really been?"

"He's been missing you like crazy, but he said that he understood your feelings and respected you for them."

"Jeez, what a guy, huh?"

"Yes, you both are like that. What have you been up to these past few days? You must have pretty much been incognito, considering that article. I am so sorry about that, but I swear, none of us wrote it, which begs the question, who did? And why? Hunter says this shows it was an inside job. It would have to be, how else would they have known how to run the machines and print the copies of the paper."

"That's clever and logical. It also makes really good sense. Any theories on how this person, or group were able to get our private conversation?"

"Hunter was pretty certain his room was bugged, so instead of tearing it apart and stomping on it, he decided to leave it alone and use it against them. We've been funneling information through his room, false of course, going out into the world, harmless. Detective Stone and his squad have been working tirelessly, trying to catch the guilty party or parties in the act."

"Jeez, that's really something. Chris, Bud and Sam have all still been in jail since beating up on Henry, right? The cops can't be lookin' for any of them for this stealin' of ideas, do they?"

"Stealing of ideas, I like that phrase, Elliot. You do have a way with words."

"Thanks, it's nice to be recognized for originality. Most people look at actors as brainless, pretty people."

"Not me, I've always thought I would never be able to learn all those pages of dialog. I wouldn't remember what my screen name was, ha ha. I've always had great respect for your profession."

The statuesque waitress walked over to top off our coffees and noticed we hadn't touched them. "Sorry, I didn't even realize you'd put the cups on the table."

"Yes, my friend and I were so busy talking, I'm afraid we're a little ignorant of what's going on around us," Robin admitted,

"Hey, that's okay. If I had someone that beautiful sitting with me, I wouldn't have noticed the coffee either," the server said with a shy smile.

"Aww, see Elliot, you've still got it!"

"Actually, I was speaking of you, ma'am," she blushed and hurried to the next table.

Both Robin and I turned a few shades of red. "Well, see Robin, you've still got it, too."

As I said this out loud to Robin, I heard my name called. It was faint but Robin heard it too, the proof of that was on her face as we both began to search through a sea of faces.

"There he is, Joe over here!" Robin jumped up, waved frantically and called to the detective.

"Over here, Joe," I called to him as well. "Thanks, you two. Jeez, it sure is busy in here this afternoon."

"You got more evidence there, Joe?" Robin asked indicating the manila envelope the good detective carried under his arm.

"Ah, yeah, I found something, but we need to go somewhere private to talk about this."

Robin and I looked at each other, then over at Joe. This situation was getting worse by the minute. "Why don't we go over to the hospital and use one of those conference rooms."

"Good idea, Elliot," Stone replied as he pulled a few bills from his pants' pocket and tossed them on the table.

We all walked out and I for one continually pivoted my head watching, looking, and observing every person in the place, each one a potential suspect.

I stopped at the Nurses' station to find out Henry's status, while the others loitered around waiting for me. I got the scoop and gathered everyone around. "He's still in surgery, but they're wrapping it up and he'll be in recovery in less than an hour. Nurse York also said we could visit briefly, like just pop our heads in the door and leave, until tomorrow."

"What a relief, thanks, Elliot."

"I didn't want to get anyone upset, but I was concerned how long it was taking," Joe admitted.

"Yeah, that's true, but Robin and I had been told it was going to take at least three to four hours, so that part didn't bother me. Well, not too much!"

I looked down the hall and saw someone walking slowly, yet purposefully. As she moved closer, I recognized Dr. Jewett. She looked utterly exhausted, yet content. There was a peace in her eyes that was reassuring and lifted my spirits.

"From the look on your face, Dr. I think you have some good news?"

"Yes, I do, Elliot. Hunter's surgery, although extremely long and tedious, went like clockwork. We will need to wait until he is fully awake before deciding if he needs another surgery, but so far, he's done extremely well. As I said earlier, you are all welcome to pop your heads in for a quick look at him, then everyone out until tomorrow!"

"Thanks, Doc" Can you take us to him?"

"I can take you," Nurse York said. "Please follow me."

The nurse opened the door and three heads popped in to look at the sleeping man.

"That's a huge bandage covering the side of his face," Robin observed.

"That's to protect *The Eye* completely, the doctor doesn't want him moving it around too much before it's had time to heal," Nurse York explained.

"His color looks good. A bit pale, but otherwise pretty healthy." Robin said and I had to agree.

"Everyone's had a chance to see him, now let's quietly leave. You can all visit tomorrow, one at a time."

"Thank you, Nurse. We all appreciate your help," Joe said.

"Detective, you said you had something to go over with us. There's an empty conference room down the hall. They only ever use it on Monday mornings, why don't we head in there."

"Yes, let's get this over with as quickly as possible."

The three of us marched into the room, shut the door and all sat down. We stared at each other and I for one definitely sat with a false sense of bravado.

"As the two of you know, Hunter was tracking a backstory of your early days, Elliot."

"Yeah, I think we're all aware of that ole chestnut."

"Elliot's right, it's in the past, or at least we're trying to get it behind us."

"What is it, Joe? There's a new development, isn't there? Did you find something more about my parents?"

"Yes, there is. I was going through the boxes of information and starting to categorize it all when I found these two photos stuck at the bottom of the box. Take a look at this girl," Joe said while pointing to an angelic face. She didn't look a day over eighteen, long strawberry blonde hair and huge, sparkling blue eyes.

"She looks somewhat familiar," Robin observed.

"Yes, she does," Elliot agreed. "I think she looks like - ; Oh, no," Elliot whispered.

"What?" asked Robin.

"Robin, she looks just like Henry."

"What are you saying?"

"I'm saying, my parents killed Henry's mother. That's right, isn't it Joe?"

"All the evidence points to it, right down to her maiden name and the fact that you can't deny Hunter looks just like her."

"I agree, I just, I don't know where to go with these feelings. I'm guilt-ridden inside, I can't imagine what he's going to go through when he finds out, and he is going to find out just as soon as the doctor says he's strong enough because I'm going to tell him."

"I know you're right, Elliot, I wish, well-"

"You wish to keep it from him, forever. But, Robin, a lie of omission is still a lie and unacceptable. Henry needs to hear the truth, and I think it'd be best coming from us."

"I agree and I feel ashamed that I even suggested he not be told, it's just that –"

"I get it, Robin. I feel the same way, but I think the last couple of months have really shown us that we need to be open and honest with each other."

"You are so right, Elliot. Let's talk with Dr. Jewett and kind of feel her out as to what Hunter could handle at this point. We may have to wait a couple of days."

"That's fine with me. Hopefully, this won't leak out all over."

"The cops were supposed to be sweeping these rooms constantly, looking for bugs. Detective Stone said there is an undercover cop here too. Apparently, she's a nurse as well so she can blend right in."

As Robin and I were talking, there was a slight knock.

"Hello Doc, come on in. Can you tell us how Henry is doing?"

"Of course, Elliot. He's resting comfortably at the moment. You can go in to see him tomorrow. We won't know about his eyesight until then, but the operation went smoothly."

"We have some, um, news to tell him and it will be a shock. We were wondering how much he could take. I mean would it set him back from healing if he gets some bad news?" Robin asked timidly.

"I would think it would depend on what the news was. He's got a very strong constitution, it would take a lot to upset him, or at least that's my opinion."

"Thanks, Dr. Jewett. That makes me feel better about the whole situation."

"Nothing for us to do until the morning, Elliot. I think I'll go into the office and get some work done. Woolridge hasn't bothered me at all since this whole thing with Hunter started, but I still have stories to get out and deadlines to meet."

"Sounds good, Robin. I'm going to grab something to eat and catch up on my sleep, so I'll look my best for Henry in the morning."

"Talk later then, we'll meet right here, around eleven am?"

"Yes, Elliot, right here is fine."

Chapter Eleven

Do You Want the Bad News or the Worse News First?

I awoke with a jolt in a sea of confusion. Everything was blurry and I hadn't a clue where I was or how I'd gotten here. There was something terribly wrong with my eye, I couldn't see at all out of it and the more awake I became, the more pain I felt.

As I was trying to decide on my next move, I heard footfalls approaching. "Hello, Hunter. How are you feeling?"

I was flooded with relief when I recognized her face. "Hello, Rachel. I'm feeling kinda out of it and I'm in quite a bit of pain. Could I possibly get something for it?"

"Yes, I'll call the nurse right now. I'd like to examine your eye since I'm right here," Dr. Jewett said as she reached for the call button.

"I'm afraid I'm having some memory issues. I know I can't see out of it, but I can't for the life of me remember what happened."

"Let me start the exam and see how much comes back to you. It really is better if you remember on your own, even if it takes longer."

As the doctor removed the bandages, chunks of memories tumbled from my mind, like slabs of snow and ice from an avalanche. Dr. Jewett worked quietly, and my memories became more and more vivid and alive.

"Okay, doc. I have my wits about me now. I remember everything that happened."

"Let me get the rest of these bandages off of you and we'll see how well you can see."

Dr. Jewett finished and had me keep my eyes shut. When she finished, she told me to open my eyes. I was nervous, so I slowly opened the good eye to make sure I could see and then I opened the other one. It was a bit blurry at first, but after blinking a few times, I was able to see clearly from both eyes.

"I'm going to page Dr. Radner. She was my assistant in your operation. I'll have her check you out too. Everything looks good, how does it feel to you?"

"It feels fine, no pain now and I can see great."

"No blurriness?"

"Not at all, doc."

"Wonderful, but I still want Amy to check you out."

"Sure, whatever you think best. Do you know when Elliot and Robin are coming to see me?"

"They should be here soon; Robin called a while ago to see if you were ready for visitors."

"Oh, that's good. It feels like forever since I've seen them."

Right then my cellphone went off.

"Hello?"

"Hi Hunter, how're you feeling?"

"Hey Robin. I'm okay, be better if you guys get here soon."

"Um, yeah, about that. We're coming, but we got tied up with something and it's going to be a bit longer than we thought."

"Oh, alright, but you are coming, right?"

"Yes, we'll just be later than we said. We'll explain everything when we get there, okay?"

Okay, then. See you later."

...

"Are you sure, Joe? I mean one hundred thirty percent sure?"

"Yes, Elliot. We have positively identified her. It's Carolyn Beecher Wilson."

"H – How am I going to tell him this? What will he think of me? What will it do to him, to us? What does this mean for me?"

"Meaning?" Joe inquired.

"My parents, my biological parents, were full-fledged, card carrying, psychotic serial killers! What about me? Do I have the gene? Am I gonna wake up one day and have a taste for murder?"

"Easy, Elliot, I don't think it works that way," Robin interjected.

"Me either, Robin," Joe added.

"How can I be sure? And now, Henry's mother? He'll never speak to me again."

"The signs would have appeared by now but if you're that worried, we can do a special test on your brain."

"Yes, Joe, I've seen that. It focuses on the pre-frontal area of the brain which controls aggression, concentration and regulates impulse control," Robin concurred.

"And if I have this thing, what then? I get locked up?"

"They maybe have meds to keep a person from murder"

"Yeah, I'm sure you're right, Robin."

I had to get out of there. I was starting to lose it, thinking I could kill someone, especially

Robin or Henry. I needed time to think before I went to tell Henry. I excused myself and told Joe and Robin I had to think about everything.

After my overreaction, I put myself in Henry's shoes and realized it was much worse for him finding out about his own mother's death. Pulling myself together, I called Robin and told her I was headed for the hospital and why didn't she join me. We met up in the parking lot and walked in the main entrance together.

Heading towards the elevator, Robin grabbed my hand. "What's up?"

"I'm thinking maybe you should do this alone. I'm not dumping you or anything, but this is private and might be better coming just from you."

I couldn't resist, I had to give her a huge hug. "Thank you, Robin. You're a good friend. I didn't want to say anything."

"It's fine, Elliot. You go alone. Text me when you're ready and I'll come say hello. I'm going to go do some shopping for now."

I waved to her as the elevator doors closed and I had a moment with my thoughts. I didn't know how to tell him. Just out with it, I guess.

All the way down to his room, I heard the death march.

Time virtually stopped as I walked into his room. His eyes were closed, and he laid there like some ancient god. His auburn hair against the pure white pillowcase was striking. Nothing could have been more sensual, then he opened his eye. I drew in my breath so quickly, I thought I would pass out.

"Hey, you. Glad you're here. Come closer so I can really see you."

"Good to see you, too Henry. I got here as soon as Robin called." I was nervous and I felt he was picking up on it.

"Where is Robin?"

"She thought we could use some alone time."

"Ha ha, that's Robin! Sounds like a good idea to me, how about you?"

"Oh, I'm all for that."

I reached out gently and stroked his cheek with my hand and felt his hot skin under my fingers. He turned toward me and the passion I saw was searing my flesh to his. I belonged to this man. No matter what happened, I was his.

"Elliot, what's goin' on in that beautiful head of yours? I can feel you thinking all the way over here."

"Henry, we're all alone, shh, let's pretend we're on a deserted island." I'd moved my body over to his bed and scooched right into him. Henry sighed and moved over just a smidgen - just enough to allow me access to him; it felt heavenly.

I cupped his chin in my hand and stroked his cheek. It felt so natural with his growing stubble.

"Elliot, you feel so nice, babe. You smell good too," Henry added. Then he told me not to fall off the fuckin' bed.

"I'll try to stay on it, thanks Henry. You smell very, uhm, clean."

"I know, it's bad, it's disinfectant and nothing gets rid of that smell."

"Maybe when you can shower."

"Only if you bring me something good smelling."

"I can do that."

"Good, now you wanna tell me what's wrong? We haven't know each other long but I feel know you well. We've been through a lot in a small-time frame. Out with it, Elliot Scott."

"Okay, okay," I sighed. Resting my head on Henry's shoulder, and wrapping my arm across his chest, I began.

"Henry, Joe discovered a couple more pictures down at the bottom of the box that he'd missed. They were of a striking young woman named, Carolyn Beecher Wilson."

I stopped and held my breath and waited. He'd been caressing my hand, then, nothing.

"Henry? Did you hear what –"

"Yeah, yeah, I heard ya. Are you certain? My dad told me my mother died in a car crash and she was carrying me. She sacrificed her life so that I would live. Are you sure of this information?"

He looked so depressed, like someone just ripped his heart out.

"Yes, Henry, we're sure, it's your Mom."

"Hi guys," Robin said quietly.

"Hi, Robin." I said.

Looking at Henry, knowing he'd wanted to be with me a fraction of a second ago, but now? Now what?

"Elliot, I'd like to talk to Robin alone please."

"Okay, I'll wait in the hallway."

"You don't have to wait. We'll be a while. You can leave."

"Alright, I'll talk with you later on. Bye, Robin."

"Bye, Elliot. I'll call you later," she said with a wan smile.

I could feel the emotions coming on and I just wanted to make it to my car. My eyes stung with unshed tears and my chest burned.

I sat in my car for a good ten minute bawling like a baby. Henry hates me. He fuckin' hates me. I thought about going home, but there was nothing there for me. Leave just leave town. With nothing but the clothes on my back, my cellphone in my back pocket and my debit card, I headed straight for the town limits. Next sign read, Welcome to Glendale, CA. I turned the car east towards Arizona and Nevada. After careful consideration, of about five seconds, I decided on Nevada.

Chapter Twelve
What Have I Done?

"Robin, I was just told something horrid. I can't even imagine it. I don't know where to put myself."

"Elliot told you about your mother?"

"You know."

"Yeah, Joe told both of us, he thought it would be easier somehow coming from us. I decided it'd be better coming from Elliot. It would give you more private time."

"That was sweet of you, girl. It's me, it's so hard for me to wrap my head around this. It's not real. Why would my dad lie about it for all those years? Who was he trying to protect? Mom was dead, nothing was gonna hurt her, so me then? How did it help anything thinking it was an accident?"

"I can't say what your dad was thinking. Apparently, he thought it was for the best. What happened with Elliot? He didn't look good when he left here."

"My fault, I blamed the messenger. I was so freaked out by what he told me, I dismissed him. Man, I really screwed up."

"How about we call him and have him come back? He'll probably just be getting home now."

"You always know the right thing to say. Thanks, Robin."

Robin tried a few times, but Elliot's phone went straight to voice mail. Before we could speculate further, Dr. Jewett walked in.

"Hello, Doc. From your face, I'd say you have some good news."

"I do indeed, Hunter. Hello, Robin. How are you doing?"

"Doing well, especially if you're handing out good news."

"All the X-rays and tests show we're on the right track. I want the bandages left on for the next twenty-four hours," Rachel said with authority as she checked under the gauze.

"Depending how it looks, you may be able to go home soon after the bandages are taken off. I would like to know you would have someone with you."

"Me!" Robin piped up. I laughed but with a twinge of guilt wishing it was Elliot saying it.

The next twenty-four hours flew by, and I hardly had time to think about anything, though thoughts of a blonde hair, dimples and honey skin managed to creep into my sleep.

Joe Stone stopped by on official business. Elliot's friends, Chris, Bud , and Sam, I preferred calling them The Lead Pipe Gang, we're coming up for trial. I'd had enough hate and wanted it to end. With Elliot not here, I didn't want it, didn't have it in me. I told Detective Stone to drop the charges. I had to write a letter which Robin helped me with.

"All right, if you're sure and by the way, I've been over to Elliot's several times. No one has seen him since the last time you saw him. They say his car is gone, but nothing else is missing."

"I can't believe he'd take off like that, although I was pretty freaked out and I was kinda rude. How is your secret investigation going?" I whispered.

"We got him this morning. My undercover detective caught him hoisting intel equipment from a ceiling panel in the doctor's lounge."

"Who is he?"

"A no-good bum named Casey that's a nobody, but, um, he works for Mr. Stanley Woolridge," Joe said then waited.

"Woolridge? My Woolridge? Jeez Joe, I can't take much more," I said pensively.

"I know, kid. It's tough. Seems he was selling you out."

"Which is why I just resigned," Robin announced from the doorway.

"Oh, Robin, c'mere," I said, arms wide. She melted into me, and I held her and rocked quite a while.

Backing away an inch, she said, "When are you being sprung?"

"Tomorrow," I exclaimed, almost happily.

"Great we can go home together," Robin replied.

"Are you sure about those boys?" Joe inquired.

"Yeah, I'm sure they learned a valuable lesson being locked up. Besides, they were protecting Elliot after all."

The day shone bright with lots of promise. No smog, heavenly blue skies and a scent of freedom in the air. Dr. Jewett had removed my bandages early and gave me a mirror to show how slight a scar I had.

I was eternally grateful for everything she'd done for me, to everyone at the hospital, but I couldn't make myself be happy. I missed Elliot too much and being honest, I was feeling guilty. I had no right to take it all out on him. If it wasn't for my snooping, he'd have no idea who his biological parents were. How could I have the nerve to dump on him. No wonder he took off.

Nobody had seen him since that day he was here, with me. Joe'd put out an APB but so far, no luck. I figured he left town. This was a hot item in Hollywood. He was recognized no matter where he went, unless disguised. Problem was, Elliot had hundreds of disguises to choose from. He could be anywhere or anybody.

I let Robin fuss over me when she came at ten to take me home. Dr. Jewett gave me a book of do's and don'ts, which Robin grabbed so fast out of my hand I got a paper cut.

"Don't worry, Doc. I'll read these cover to cover and make sure he follows it to the letter," Robin said emphatically.

"I'm sure you will, Robin. Good luck, Hunter. Your follow up appointment is in that packet; I look forward to seeing you. If you need anything at all before your scheduled, please come in and see me."

"I will Doc and I look forward to seeing all of you. It's still hard seeing only half a face."

"Yes , but I think leaving the bandages on will help *The Eye*. Take it off several times a day and do the exercises. You should start to feel improvement."

Giving Rachel a big hug, I said a tearful goodbye, got in the regulation wheelchair and Robin and I were off.

"You wanna stop for a bite, or a coffee?"

"Nah, let's just go home."

"Alrighty then."

We traveled in silence the rest of the way. She parked in the driveway behind a black SUV.

"Hum, wonder who's here?"

"Don't know, guess we'll find out."

Robin went for the bags as my door flew open and there stood Joe, all six-foot seven inches of him.

"Welcome home! Here, Robin, let me grab those, you help our patient."

I balked at that, "I'm not a patient! See, got my walking papers today," I shouted as I jammed my release papers in Joe's face, which made everyone laugh.

"Good for you, least I know you're not AWOL."

Walking into my house felt weird. It seemed ages since I was there. It smelled of pine, lemon and bleach. Robin's doing, no doubt.

"Here Hunt, let's get you settled, and I'll make a bite of something for all of us. Joe, you will stay, yes?

"Yes, if it's okay with Hunter."

"Of course, Joe. You're always welcome."

"Thanks. Now do you want an update on those three you let go?"

"How are they doing?"

"They say they're remorseful and grateful to you for dropping the charges. Chris, especially seems truly sorry."

"You sound skeptical. Have a little faith. I think they'll do fine and won't act up again. Plus, they were protecting Elliot."

"I'm a cop, it's my job to be distrustful," Detective Stone said with a grimace.

"You're doing your job extremely well, my friend."

"Hunter, you sure you don't want me to put another APB out on Elliot? I can do it easily."

"Yeah, I know you can, but I don't want him here because he was dragged back. I want him to want to be here with me. I'm afraid I fucked up and it's gonna take him time to think it all through. But I feel I should get some leeway too. It was my mother that got,um, killed and my dad lying to me all those years. I mean, what is that?"

Robin walked in with a huge tray filled with chicken soup and thick grilled cheese sandwiches.

"Let me take the tray, Robin."

"Thanks, Joe. It was a bit touch and go for a while."

"Hunter, after you eat, it's off to bed with you."

"Yeah, okay. I'm feeling tired."

I couldn't eat a lot; my stomach was upset, and I really was sleepy. "Okay Robin, I'm ready to go to bed."

"I'll be right down, Joe. Let's go Hunt."

Three months later

I've been recovering nicely and got a job on The Los Angeles Times. I'm really happy to be working on a respectable newspaper. The best thing about it is Robin works there too. Truth is, she put in a good word for me.

My life is simple, which is just fine with me, but I can't help but wonder about Elliot.

I was so upset about my mom that day. I was so rude to him. I haven't heard word one from him since that day.

It's my one big regret in this life. I miss him every day as I wake up alone, make my dinner alone, watch TV alone. Robin helps with much of it, but sitting at my new desk right now, I can't help but wish. I could share with Elliot.

"Hey Wilson, how's it going? You settling in alright?" Obadiah Bond asked.

" I'm doing good, man. Everyone's been great here."

"Yeah it's a good team."

"Did you have a good week end?"

" Oh man, did we ever. Took the wife to Vegas for the entire weekend."

"Nice. Win big?"

"Broke even, more or less ha ha. But the best part by far was who we saw working there."

"Really, who was it?"

"That superstar movie actor, Elliot Scott. Jeez man, you okay?

" Yeah, yeah," I said as I jumped up from my desk as the hot coffee spread over my legs.

"Better be careful, friend. You just got back to work."

"Right so tell me, are you sure it was him; I mean without a doubt?"

"Positive."

"Where was he working?"

" Get this, he's a blackjack dealer at the Luxor Hotel and Casino."

"The Luxor? Isn't that the huge pyramid?"

"Yup. It was fantastic there. I asked Elliot if he was preparing for a new role, and he gave me his autograph."

"Wow, good for you. I better go change."

"Talk later pal."

Oh my God! I ran straight to the men's room to put cold water on my thighs and privates. I could barely turn the faucet on, my hands shook so much, and my heart was pounding out of my chest. Obadiah wasn't the sharpest tool in the shed, but he wasn't dumb, nor did he lie. If he says he got Elliot's autograph, he did.

Elliot was in Las Vegas, roughly two hundred seventy miles from here. I could be there in four, maybe five hours. "I have to get Robin," I mumbled as I dashed from the men's room like a crazy person; trousers still wet with coffee and water.

I spotted Robin talking to a few other people. I must have startled her running up and grabbing her hand and yelling "Come with me!"

"Hunter, what is it? Are you sick? You're hyperventilating, slow down your breathing. Are you in pain? I'll call an ambulance."

"No," I managed to croak out. "Give me a sec."

I sat down on the hallway carpet and got a hold of myself.

"Robin, Obadiah Bond just told me he and his wife went to Vegas this weekend."

"That's what's got you practically having a stroke? Are you kidding me? You scared me to death, Hunter Wilson!"

"May I continue? Robin nodded permission and I said, "Guess who they saw in Vegas."

"From your expression, I'd say Santa Claus and the Easter Bu- oh my gosh, no!"

"Yes, it's true."

"He's sure it was Elliot?"

"He's got his autograph."

"He really is right there in Vegas. What's he doing there?"

"Working as a blackjack dealer."

"When are you leaving"

"As soon as I can book a flight, driving's too slow. You wanna come with?"

"I'd love to, but I got a deadline. How are you going to waltz out the door on a Monday morning?"

I'm gonna tell the boss I'm following a big story."

"I'm so happy you finally at least know where he is, and I understand you going but-"

"But he's known where I was this whole time and could've come to see me. Yeah, I know, but I also know he was hurt by my pushing him away and I think, he thinks, I don't want him around because of what his parents did to my mom. I can't blame him; I didn't handle it very well."

"It was a shock but yeah, I can see him getting hurt by perceiving your reaction as hostile."

"Jeez, Robin, where'd you get all that malarkey?"

"Oh funny. It's not malarkey. It's proven fact."

"Proven? By whom?"

"You know, them," Robin said, satisfied with herself.

"Oh, oh, that's right - it's them."

"You're mean, Hunter. Get out of here and go find Elliot."

"Right, Elliot. Going to talk to the boss to let him know I'm going after a big one. That's not really a lie."

I wrapped my arms around my best girl and squeezed. Kissed the top of her head and off I went.

"Hugs back, my friend. Good luck to you and give my love to Elliot."

"Will do and you take care of yourself while I'm gone."

A stop in the editor's office and I was off to bring home the love of my life or go home broken, busted, and alone.

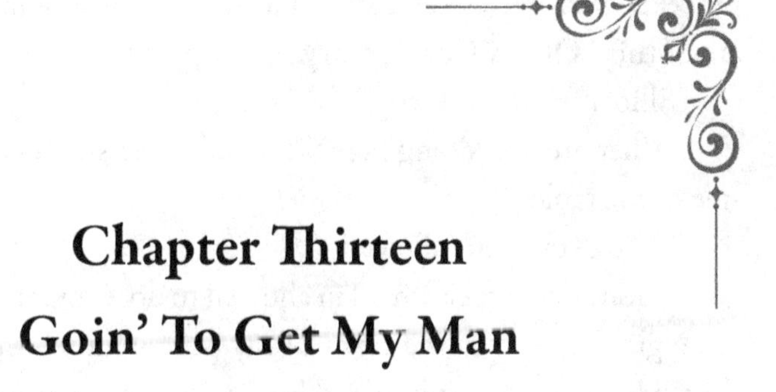

Chapter Thirteen
Goin' To Get My Man

OH, BROTHER. HERE'S another smartass thinks he knows everything about card playing in Vegas.

Honestly, I really enjoy my job, but when I get these bozos who are trying to impress everyone around them with what card sharks they are, I want to punch them out, or better yet, out them. Let the ones their playing the big cheese for find out they can't count to twenty-one.

Over on the roulette wheel, I saw my latest conquest, Ned Lawson. Even from this distance I could see his bulging biceps. And that hair. He practically sits on it. Long, shiny, straight and black. He had all the features of a perfect male specimen. Ned's a great guy in the sack, out of it, not so much. He has his set ways and won't change. We use each other for sex and the convenience factor; we're both here in the casino and back at the apartment, usually at the same time.

I really am messed up, almost four months and I still can't say my apartment, it's always The. I still have nightmares of that awful day when I had to tell Henry his mother was killed by my parents. Makes me physically ill to think about it.

With no one at my table, I was able to look around the casino and watch the patrons. Coming across the room was a very determined person. He ploughed through crowds of milling gamblers and proceeded to get closer to my table. There was something familiar about this - Oh my God. "Henry," I whispered.

"Elliot!" Henry roared.

"What are you doing here?" I asked as he stomped around to my side of the table.

"N-No, you aren't allowed -."

" I don't give a fuck what I'm allowed to do. C'mere," Henry growled as he grabbed me by the front of my pure white, button-down dress shirt. He pulled me to him and kissed me. I was enthralled, I couldn't help but kiss him back.

Suddenly, there was a flurry of activity and I realized Ned had a hold of Henry and belted him square in the nose.

"Noo, Ned, stop!" I screamed. I ran over and tried to get him off of Henry.

"Ned, I said stop! This is Henry."

"Henry?" Ned started to listen to me and loosened his grip.

"Ya mean the one that broke your heart? The one you have nightmares about? The one you cried over while I held you? That Henry?"

Henry was in a precarious spot. His nose was bleeding profusely and one wrong move at this moment, Ned would snap his neck in two.

"Elliot, I suggest a different approach," Henry said thoughtfully.

"Shut up Wilson. That's your real name, Hunter Wilson."

"You got me there, big fella. What's your name?"

"I'm Ned Lawson, that's who the fuck I am. You're putting your hands and mouth in places that don't belong to ya."

"I'm afraid you're wrong there, pal. Elliot belongs to me," Hunter claimed.

"Whoa, hold on, wait just a damn minute!" I yelled so loud everyone stopped and looked at me.

"I'm nobody's property. I belong to my own self, don't either of you forget that" I said furiously

"Elliot, we need t-."

" Yeah I know, come with me." I said while putting a hand up to Henry's swollen lips. They were hard to see through the handkerchief he had stemming the blood from his nose.

"But Elliot," Ned whined.

"Ned, go back to the roulette wheel. Maybe you'll be a big winner." I said.

"I don't like this Elliot."

"Look, Henry, I get off in two hours. Come back then and we'll talk."

"Nah, I got a better idea."

"What's that?" I asked cautiously.

"I'll stay right here at your table and play until you get off," Henry said with a twinkle in his eye.

"I can't stop you from sitting here but I can't talk now."

" I know but you won't have this job much longer anyway."

"What's that supposed to mean?"

"It means you're coming home with me. No more shenanigans."

He looked so damn cute standing there, arms akimbo, lips pursed, and tapping his foot, I couldn't help but laugh."

"Your eye looks great Henry. Dr. Jewett really knows what she's doing."

"Yes, she does and stop changing the subject."

A couple wandered over to my table and threw their money down and so did Henry. I looked across the room and there was Ned, growling from the roulette table.

Everyone played a few losing hands, then Henry won a substantial amount.

" I didn't know you really knew this game."

"There are lots of things you don't know about me." Henry said with a shit eating grin.

The next two hours dragged and flew at the same time. Dragged because I really wanted to be alone with Henry. It had been a long three months. It flew because I was scared of what would happen to us at the end of the discussion.

Finally, I was done with my shift. Henry had won over ten thousand dollars. He was immediately made a VIP and treated accordingly.

He was given the Kings Room, which included two bedrooms, a hot tub, and a huge fireplace.

"Not bad, eh Elliot?"

" Not bad at all. I've only seen this room from the brochures. I've got a tiny room downstairs. It suits me just fine. But this, Wow."

"Let's sit down and start hashing things out. You want something to eat or drink?"

"Nah, I'm too nervous to eat."

"Okay, let's start with the obvious," Henry said as he sat on the California King bed.

"I owe you an apology," Henry said with bowed head.

"You owe me? What are you talking about? I said as I followed suit and sat down next to him. Not close enough to touch, but not too far apart.

"Yes, I was rude, mean, and sarcastic when you told me about my mother. I don't blame you for wanting to get as far away from me as possible."

"You're right, I was shocked and hurt but then I thought how you must feel. Not only did I deliver the news, but it was my family that made it happen. You must have wondered what kind of monster I was; I know I was wondering myself. I was told there's a test to see if I have the predisposition for it. I've been thinking of taking it."

"Elliot, I honestly don't think you have to worry about it, but if it will ease your mind, you should do it. Now, explain why you left town. You could've gone home and stayed there. Instead you traveled hundreds of miles away. That was extreme."

"I left the hospital that day when you said you wanted to talk to Robin alone and just wanted to fall in a fault or a deep well or something. I felt horrible over what I'd done to you. I jumped in my car and started driving east. I saw the signs for Las Vegas and thought I could hide here. Which brings up a question. How did you find me?"

"You remember a fella name of Obadiah Bond? You gave him an autograph."

"It's impossible to forget Obadiah. You know him?"

"We work together, and he's proud as a peacock with that autograph. I felt like telling him he doesn't know the half of it."

"You said work. Are you still with *The Eye*? You and Robin?"

"No, remember I was fired. After the stunt Woolridge pulled, I would've quit, like Robin did."

"She really quit over that, that's nice to hear. So, what's the new job?"

" You are looking at one of the newest employees at The LA Times. It's a small job right now as they test me to see how I write and if I can write."

"Where are you, obituaries?"

"Exactly. It's not so easy cramming ones entire life into a couple of paragraphs, but it's challenging."

" I'm sorry, Henry. I was being facetious. It sounds like a lot of responsibility and I'm proud of you. Robin, where is she?"

"She's with me at The Times, but she got the Miss Lovelorn column. She loves it."

" I bet she does, she has great insight."

"Yes, she does. She says you and I are meant to be together. What do you think, Elliot?"

"All I know is when I saw you heading towards me, my heart started pounding and my throat went dry. My hands started to sweat too. You know what all that adds up to?"

"An allergic reaction?"

"Very funny, Henry. It means I'm in love with you, ya twit."

"I love you, too, Elliot. Look, we've got all this money, a beautiful suite to stay in, what's say you go quit your job and we do this town right. No gambling, just sightseeing. I'd love to see Hoover Dam."

"Are you sure? I'm worried the past, my past, will come between us."

"How can it, everything's out in the open now. The past has all been exposed. Well, except for."

"Except for what?"

"Ned Lawson."

"Oh yeah. Almost forgot about him. I thought you and I were over. Ned was a distraction. We used each other for sex, that's all it ever was."

"I'm not so sure that's it on his side. He seemed pretty shook up, especially after hitting me."

"Yeah he's usually a nice guy. I'll have a talk with him. We'll straighten it all out."

I sat quietly trying to think, when I felt hot breath on my ear, the spot that really turns me on.

"Henry, that's dirty pool."

"All's fair in love and war," Henry said as he started kissing my neck. He knows all the right places. My arms went around him, and we started kissing so intensely I wasn't sure I could hold on.

Just when I thought I might climax, there was a terrible banging on the suite doors.

"What the fuck?"

The pounding didn't stop. Henry went to the door and my boss barged in with a couple of our muscle men and Ned following behind.

"Hello Mr. Cole. What brings you here?" I asked politely.

"You do, Scott. I understand your friend here won a good amount at your blackjack table."

"Yes sir, oh this is Hen- Hunter Wilson, Hunter, my boss, Mr. Cole."

"How do you do, sir," Henry said with his hand out. Cole shook it briefly.

"I'd be doing better if I knew the two of you weren't in kahoots."

"Kahoots?" I said, flabbergasted. "You think I was cheating? Sir, I've been here three months with a perfect record. I do not cheat. And neither does Henry."

"Who is Henry?" Cole blasted.

"Hunter, Henry's a nickname." I said.

"Not in cahoots, huh? Mind telling me about that ten Grand you walked out of my casino with?"

"I was watching them, Mr. Cole. Something fishy goin' on if ya ask me," Ned chimed in.

"Ned, stay out of this. You're only saying that cuz you're jealous," I said sharply.

"Jealous? Of what? Him?" Ned replied, indicting Henry.

"I can clear this all up. My dad taught me to play blackjack before I could walk. I'm good at it, one might even say a genius at the game. I don't need to cheat or have Elliot cheat for me, and I can prove it," Henry taunted.

"How do you propose doing that?" Mr. Cole responded.

" You play me Mr. Cole. Just you and me with everyone watching and your goons can stand watch over me. What'd ya say?"

"Alright, kid. One condition, Scott can't be in the room. If you are working together, I don't want him getting signals to you," Cole grumbled

"That's fair, sorry Elliot," Henry said to me.

"That's okay. I'll go downstairs to my room.

"Thanks, Elliot. This won't take long."

I left the room reluctantly. I remembered there was a small window on the side of the door. I went to it and peeked inside.

I couldn't see much, but I did see Henry take the first game, then the second, and finally the third. Voices raised quickly.

"How did you do that? You must have been switching cards, had them up your sleeves," Mr. Cole barked.

"How could I have done that? I took off my coat and my sleeves are rolled past the elbows. Plus, I haven't so much as touched the cards and the goons have their eagle eyes on me. I told you, I'm that good at blackjack." Henry said.

"I'm beginning to think I've been wasting my time."

" I swear, Mr. Cole, I saw them cheating," Ned whined.

"Ned, you and I are going to have a little talk."

"Yes, sir," Ned said dejectedly.

"Mr. Wilson, Hunter, I owe you an apology. You have one night comped I'm giving you a second. Here are vouchers for the formal dining room - order anything you want on the menu."

"Thank you, sir. That's very gracious of you," Henry said.

"Yes, sir. We really appreciate it," I added.

I hurried around the corner and knocked on Henry's door. One of Mr. Cole's henchmen let me in.

"Elliot, take tomorrow off and show your friend around, Mr. Cole smiled."

Henry and I looked at each other and I knew this was it. Even though it hadn't been smooth sailing throughout the relationship, I felt the heart finds the truth and for us it was we were meant to be together.

"Again, thank you, Mr. Cole." We said in unison.

Ned was fit to be tied and stormed from the room. I'd talk with him later, he needed time to cool down.

"Well, Henry what should we do first?"

"I think we should get rid of all these people."

"I like your way of thinking. Okay, Mr. Cole, boys it's been great, but I think we can handle it from here."

"We're leaving," said the goons together.

"Enjoy your stay, Mr. Wilson, Elliot," Mr. Cole held his hand out.

"Sir," I said as I shook his hand.

"Thank you, Mr. Cole," Henry said following my lead.

"I thought they'd never leave," Henry complained as he shut and locked the door.

I was getting a fluttering in my stomach that was warming the lower half of my anatomy. My cock started to come alive, the closer Henry got. It was as if he knew it and was going slow on purpose to get me heated up.

I was sitting on the edge of the bottom of the bed. Henry came closer and closer, moving slowly. He flipped his shoes off, one at a time, along his way. Next, he undid his belt, unbuttoned and unzipped his pants. That's when I saw the incredible bulge in his boxers. I thought I'd lose it right then. He bent down, put his hands on either side of my face and caressed my cheekbones with his thumbs.

"Oh, Henry, that feels so good. Don't stop."

"Never, babe. I want to spend the rest of my life pleasing you," Henry whispered in my ear.

"I'm so very sorry I ran off the way I did," I said while licking his earlobe. I had one arm around his neck, and I was removing his shirt with the other. Buttons were a hindrance, but I was up for the challenge.

"No, Elliot. It was my fault. I was so shocked by your admission, I couldn't think. That's no excuse though, and I shouldn't have shot the messenger," Henry said while kissing my eyelids, cheeks, jawbone, and lips.

I started to moan, and he pushed me down on the bed and removed my tie in one movement. My shirt disappeared next. It came off so quickly, I never saw it. I grabbed Henry's shirt and pulled it completely off of his body.

"Henry, babe, I want your hands on every inch of my body. Please, fuck me within an inch of my life."

His eyes were soft with love and longing. He cupped my face and continued to caress my cheek. I fairly melted into his hand. The sigh of contentment that escaped his throat made my cock start to fill. Our bodies melded together without either of us noticing. Mouths locked and hands sought out skin. We were breathing heavier with each passing second. Tongues twirled and intertwined, mouths and bodies followed suit.

I wrapped my left arm around Henry's neck, relishing in the warmth I found there. My right arm around his middle and smoothly worked my way around to his back with an open palm. Meanwhile, Henry's hands moved down my back until he had two plump globes of my ass to squeeze.

"Elliot, your ass is so delicious." The moans became louder and more intense as their cocks filled to the point of being uncomfortable.

"Oh God, babe, fuck me now. I need you now!" I cried.

"Whoa, I'll give you what you want, but I won't hurt you. We need to take it easy."

"I don't wanna take it easy, I want it hard and fast, now."

Henry picked up the lube and condom from where he'd thrown them on the bed. He unwrapped and rolled the condom on his thickening tool and lubed up generously, both himself and my hole.

"Just listening to you, Elliot is making me rock hard. Let me line up with your hole."

Henry lifted my legs onto his shoulders to get a better angle. I was practically incoherent with desire at this point. He began to push into me but stopped when he met with resistance. I hissed but would not be deterred. Instead of pulling away, I pushed into him until his dick was up to my balls. Henry stilled his body then and waited for me to adjust to his size. He leaned down and started licking my left nipple and gently bit until it was a hard nub. He then repeated the sensuous activity on my right nipple.

I was squirming and moaning so loudly and intensely, Henry began moving inside of me in earnest. "Oh, love, you're so tight, so hot," Henry moaned.

"I'm not gonna last, babe, I'm gonna come real soon," I warned.

"Yeah, me too, babe. You're too much."

I exploded all over our stomachs. "Elliot, you look so sexy with your reddened face and blown pupils, I can't hold on any longer." Henry came hard, and I could feel the heat from the sperm as it filled the condom deep within my bowels.

Henry collapsed on top of my heaving chest, and we stayed unmoving for a good long while.

After coming back to the living, Henry said, "Elliot, you have a beautiful body along with a beautiful soul. You're one of the purest people I have ever met. I love you, Elliot Scott."

"Henry, that was lovely. We've been through a lot since we met, which was also under unusual circumstances. But we've weathered them all and I believe we're stronger for it. I love you too Henry Hunter Wilson. Will you marry me?"

Henry stopped kissing me long enough to watch me for a good thirty seconds. A smile slowly crept over his face, his thick auburn mop in delicious disarray. Then the smile faded, but the sparkle in his eyes brightened. "Yes, Elliot Scott, I will marry you."

My heart leapt in my chest, and I grinned from ear to ear. Henry bent all the way down and kissed me oh so tenderly on the lips. He began to probe with his tongue, and we used them to fight for dominance.

Henry crawled down my body to my dick. He began kissing and licking it briefly, then suddenly, he engulfed the entire meaty piece in one swoop.

"Wow! Oh, man. Jeez, babe, that was amazing."

"Like that huh?" Henry asked.

"Oh, yeah."

"Thought you would."

"I'm close, babe. Faster, harder, ohh, don't stop," I yelled.

Henry listened very well. He did go faster and harder. I was about there. "Ohhhh, I love you Henry Hunter Wilson."

"Ha Ha, I love that!"

Now was my turn to reciprocate. I flipped us over, so he was under me, and I gave him the same treatment he'd just given me.

I couldn't get enough of him. I kissed his hair, lips, ears, eyebrows, cheekbones, neck, nose. All slowly and sensually.

"Oh, Elliot, oh you sure know what you're doing. Oh, fuck."

I had taken ahold of his cock while kissing his chest. I developed an even rhythm and Henry moved along with it. He had a look of pure bliss and I felt triumphant. He was moaning and writhing back and forth. Henry grabbed my hair and pulled me down for another thrilling kiss. He started to hump up and down erratically and then, "Elliot, I'm gonna blow! Ah ,ah, oh."

All I heard was heavy breathing. I wrapped my arms around him and held him close, giving him feathery kisses.

"Elliot, that was surreal. Here let me roll over."

Henry licked and kissed me from my jawline straight down my chest, stomach and then down to my cock. He used that incredible tongue of his until I was ready to lose my mind.

"Henry, please, suck on me, faster, babe. I'm going crazy here. Please, more."

"Like this?" he asked while sucking on my rock-hard dick.

"Oh, I'm coming, Henry, oh shit."

We curled up together and fell asleep.

Chapter Fourteen
Another County Heard From

"HENRY," A VOICE WHISPERED.

"Mm?"

"Henry," a voice raised.

"Mm, yeah? What is it?"

"Time to get up now."

"Huh? Who's there?" I said, fully awake now. I turned the light on and cringed. Standing over me was Ned Lawson, a gun in his left hand.

"Ned? What are you doing? You don't want to use that."

"Yeah, actually I do. I'm gonna shoot your lover there, the one that jilted me, then I'm gonna shoot you, and then myself."

"But, if you shoot yourself, you can't enjoy our deaths."

"If I don't shoot myself, the cops will haul my ass off to jail."

"The cops don't even know you're here and we won't tell them."

"Of course, you won't, you'll be dead. What I look, stupid?"

"No, not in the least. But you gotta think this through. Like you said, the cops will probably be on you, so if you don't shoot us, no cops and you'll be in the clear."

"But I gotta shoot ya. Elliot hurt me really bad and you're the reason he did it. I need to get rid of both of you."

I kept moving over little by little trying to protect Elliot. I felt him moving but wasn't sure if he were awake and I couldn't take the chance to look at him.

"Ned, where did you get the gun?"

"I've had it a while. Ever since I figured out Elliot just wanted me for sex."

"Isn't that what you wanted, too?"

"Nah, I wanted a relationship with him. He wouldn't give in to me, too much in love with you, Mr. Pretty Boy."

"It's time for this to come to an end. How do ya want it? I can kill you right where you're lying, or you can get out of the bed and face me. I can shoot you standing up like a man."

Having virtually no choice, I moved slowly away from Elliot.

"That's it, another inch and –"

Bam Crash Snap Boom

"Ned Lawson, hands on top of your head, now!"

"Put the gun down, slowly."

"Who the fuck are you?"

"We're the fuckin' police, that's who we are and you're under arrest for breaking and entering, threatening people with a loaded weapon, attempted murder, and anything else we can come up with. I'm Officer Styles, by the way."

Elliot really had been awake and had dialed 911 under the covers. "My hero," I croaked.

"It wasn't much of anything, Henry. I heard what was going on and scared Ned was going to shoot you. I can't believe I misjudged him so much. I never thought he'd become violent, not in a million years."

"Goes to show nobody really knows anybody," said Styles. "You two sure you're okay? We're going to need you down the station to make statements."

"Yes, sir. We'll be ready," Henry replied.

"Ditto."

After everyone had gone, Elliot and I sat quietly wrapped in each other's arms and the warm, fluffy robes left for us by management.

"Guess we'd better start getting ready to go to the station," Elliot remarked.

"Mm, just a few more minutes of this, then we'll go."

"No, let's go now or we never will. You go jump in the shower and I'll get clothes out."

"Boy, we just got engaged and you're already taking over," I complained, but with a smile.

"Damn right, somebody has to," Elliot replied with a smirk. "Move it, now."

"I'm going, I'm going, hey," I stopped.

"Yeah?"

"I love you."

"Love you, too."

We somehow made it down to police headquarters within the hour and gave our statements to the officers. It took longer than we thought, so we stopped for a bite to eat on the way back to the hotel.

"We need to call Robin and let her know what's going on. The last she knew I was coming here to find you."

"Yeah, let's call her as soon as we get back to the room," Elliot said with a mouth full of chili fries.

"Hello?"

"Hey girl. Sorry it took so long to call. Things have been jumping here."

"Thank goodness you called. Did you find Elliot?"

"Not only did I find him but, hang on to your panties, we're getting married!"

"What? OH my God. I have to hear this, no wait, put Elliot on."

"Hi, Robin."

"Oh, it's so good to hear your voice. You are in so much trouble, mister for running away like that. Family stays and fights it out, it never runs away."

"Yes, that's been drilled into me now. I'm sorry I worried you."

"I'm just glad you're alright and, wow, getting married. I bet you asked Hunter, huh?"

"Yeah, but how'd you know?"

"I just know. I am going to be in the wedding, right?"

"Of course. We were thinking maid of honor/best man, what d'ya think?"

" I love it. When are you coming home so we can make plans?"

"Soon, love. We have to tie up some loose ends here first," I said.

" Great. Safe travels home. See you both soon. Love you."

"Love you, too," We said in unison.

"I'd better go break the news to Mr. Cole. I'm sure he can replace me in no time."

"I don't know, babe. I think he's really gonna miss you. He likes you a lot," I said.

"He likes having a face people recognize. It draws them to my table, so he makes more money. Except when you're playing," Elliot said laughingly.

"What can I say, some's got it, and some's don't. My dad taught me every way to win at blackjack known to man and it stuck."

"Sure, glad it did. Speaking of which, I gotta go clean out my room downstairs. Not that there's much in it, but I have a couple of company uniforms that will need to be turned in and a few personal items. I'll go talk to Mr. Cole now then get my stuff. You wanna meet back here and then head out?"

"Yeah, that'll work. We only have a couple things to pack here. Just close up the suitcase and I'm done."

"You think they'd miss a couple of those robes?" Elliot asked innocently.

"Why, I don't think they'd mind at all. I'll get 'em stuffed in the suitcase before you get back," I assured Elliot.

With a peck on my cheek, Elliot was out the door. At least this time I didn't have a sense of foreboding or doom and gloom. I was feeling on Cloud Nine when it hit me.

I'd told my editor I needed some time to explore a great story. What would I tell him when I got back? He'd probably fire me for wasting his and the paper's time. I sat down at the table trying to think off what to do and that's precisely where Elliot found me forty-five minutes later.

"Henry? Hey, you okay, babe? Why so lost in thought? Are you having second thoughts about us?"

"Huh, no, no not about us, never about us. I do have a problem though."

I proceeded to tell Elliot about my situation.

"That's an easy fix, Henry. Tell your editor the truth. You followed a love story to Las Vegas, and it ended up with a reunion and a wedding proposal."

"Now why didn't I think of that," I shook my head. "Maybe you should write the story."

"No way, you're the writer in this family. I'm the one who interprets the words and creates life from the written page."

"Sounds like two halves make a whole. I like it."

"Mm, I'm not sure I'm happy with the way it is. Starting a new life with you, makes me wonder if I can or even want to go back to my old life."

"I think our lives are all made up by blending the old and the new. I was contemplating the same thing. What if you sell your place and I give notice and move out of mine, and we buy a new place that will be ours. Maybe near the ocean," I offered.

"I think that's a brilliant idea, Henry. I'll get on it as soon as we get home. I'm sure my real estate guy can get a good price and could also show us some new places. No wonder I love you. I'm marrying a genius," Elliot said pridefully.

"I wouldn't go that far unless you're talking blackjack. I'll take merely brilliant, thank you."

"Looks like you've got everything from the room, and I've got this small bag from my room. Let's get this show on the road," Elliot said with gusto.

"First, let's have one for the road," I said as I slid my arms around Elliot, and he did the same. We kissed gently and deeply, hugged then grabbed our gear and out the door.

Once outside, a valet brought my car around. We hopped in and I drove to Elliot's car.

"See ya back in LA." Elliot said with a wave.

"Where do you want to meet? I asked but suddenly knew.

"Robin's," we said in chorus.

We wouldn't stop until we got there.

Chapter Fifteen

So, You Thought You'd Get a Happy Ending Now?

Gliding down Route 15, looking at the scenery, which wasn't much to look at out in the desert, I couldn't keep the smile off my face. Married. I'm getting married. And to the best person on the planet. Man, I really am crazy about that guy.

I noticed some black puffs rising from the road further up. Looks like an accident, hope Elliot didn't get caught in it. I heard the sirens and saw emergency vehicles disregarding the median strip dividing northbound and southbound traffic areas to get to the scene quickly. All traffic on my side was forced to slow down, then stop. There were only about ten of us so the police directing traffic, had cones up and got us moving in short order.

I started to get a cold, clammy feeling in the pit of my stomach, like thousands of tendrils were floating around in my gut.

I couldn't help the gawk factor as I rode up to the accident. There was a mass of metal melded into metal. It was barely discernable there had been two cars present. It was one smashed ball of car parts. A bright yellow tarp lay on the asphalt covering some poor person and the rescue units were gathered around another hunk of vehicle, shouting out orders and using the jaws of life.

Jeez, what a mess. As I was passing by the end of it, something caught my eye. Lying on the side of the road was, no it couldn't be, but yes it was, Elliot's duffel bag. I'd know it anywhere. It was old and ratty and one of the handles was falling off, but he loved it.

What would Elliot's bag be do-.

I flew to the side of the road and stopped my car. My brain was numb, and my limbs felt like fifty-pound weights were strapped to them. I slowly opened my door with shaking hands and walked over towards the emergency crew.

"Whoa now, hold on there, buddy. You can't be here. Get back in your car and take off," the traffic cop told me.

"I think my fiancé is in that car. His bag is up there on the road," I said, pointing.

"Was he driving out here today?"

"Yeah, we both were. We were in Las Vegas and left in separate cars to go back home to LA. Please, I need to find out, please let me go," I begged. I was feeling weaker by the second.

"Here, son, sit down. You're not looking so hot."

He had me sit in his patrol car on the median. "I'll see what I can find out for you. What's your name?"

"Hunter Wilson."

"And his?"

"Elliot, Elliot Scott."

"The actor?"

"Yes, sir. Please I need to know. If it's him, I need to be there."

"Be right back."

I watched out the back window as the policeman went up to one of the rescue workers, say something, then point over to me. They exchanged a few more words, then both headed for me. My heart dropped into my stomach at this point. It was Elliot and he's dead.

"Mr. Wilson? I'm Captain Blake. The man being extracted from the vehicle is indeed Elliot Scott. I, along with two others have positively identified him."

Well thank goodness he was still identifiable. "He's dead?" I whispered.

"No, sir. He's alive, but unconscious. He's hurt awful bad, but I can't give you particulars until he's free of the car and worked on by my men."

"May I get closer? I might be able to help. I really need to see him for myself."

"Not until we have him out of there. It's not safe for you. I'll come get you. Oh, here comes the ambulance now. Excuse me," Captain Blake said as he rushed off to direct the ambulance.

"He'll be taken to Boulder City Hospital," the cop said after watching the ambulance drive up. "Why don't I take you there now. I'll have one of my officers bring your car. You don't look like you're in much shape to drive at this point. Swing your legs in the car and we'll be off," he said gently.

"But what if he wakes up scared? I should stay with him," I said, starting to panic.

"Son, I really don't think he's going to come to, yet. If you get to the hospital, you can fill out important paperwork the docs will need to help him."

"That makes sense, yeah okay we can go," I said as I kept my eyes trained on the horrible sight behind me.

"I'm Officer Vinton, by the way."

"Nice to meet you," I replied.

I was fairly a basket case by the time we got to the emergency room. Officer Vinton sat me down in a small private room off the emergency room. It was in this room doctors told of loved ones that had died. I couldn't hold on any longer. Tears began to stream down my cheeks unabated. The love of my life was dead, and they were trying to soften the blow. I felt pain like I've never felt before, not even when my mom died. This was a primal hurt, as if I'd lost my own limb. By the time Officer Vinton came in with a doctor, I was shaking uncontrollably and sobbing like a child.

"Mr. Wilson, I'm Dr. Keys. Your fiancé is being rerouted to us as we speak. He's in bad shape, but alive. Do you hear me, Mr. Wilson?"

"Y-yeah, I do. You sure he's alive?"

"I was in contact with the paramedics not five minutes ago. I need to ask you, Mr. -"

"Hunter, please doc."

"Hunter, do you hold Elliot's health proxy or have written permission to make medical decisions for him?"

"No, we had barely gotten engaged. We were on our way home to tell our friends. Elliot had only asked me to marry him three hours ago. This is a nightmare."

"I'm afraid without his consent, I won't be able to tell you much. When he wakes up, we will ask him if he wants you to know about his condition. We can legally accept a verbal response as long as it's witnessed. Don't worry, Hunter. Your fiancé is in the best care this side of the Mississippi."

Dr. Keys had a calming effect and I settled down somewhat. Officer Vinton brought me a cup of coffee and stayed with me until the doctor returned almost forty-five minutes later.

I jumped to my feet, spilling coffee on the couch and floor. "Sorry. Doc, how is he?"

"He's holding his own for now. He's given permission for you to know about his medical condition. He's awake right now but going to surgery soon. Now would be the time to see him, we can talk after, if you're agreed."

"Yes, please take me to him."

"Come with me."

I followed the doctor down a long corridor that reminded me of my hospital stay. "You can only stay for a minute, he's very weak."

"Understood. I just really need to see him for myself."

Doctor Keys left me standing outside the curtained area. I heard low murmurs but couldn't make out any actual words. He came out within ten seconds and told me to go right in. I developed cold feet in those few seconds and had to prompt myself to move one foot in front of the other. What would I find on the other side of that curtain? I was scared shitless but had to do it for Elliot. Shame on me for thinking of myself when he's the one lying in a hospital bed about to have surgery. I screwed up my courage and flung open the curtain.

He was lying on his back, but with pillows keeping him angled on his right side. His head was bandaged like a mummy in a late-night horror movie. I could see his eyes peeking out of the white gauze. His left arm was at a ninety-degree angle to his hip, which is where the arm was resting. It was strapped onto his body so he couldn't move it. His legs were hidden under the blankets, so I had no idea what shape they were in. He had tubes coming and going all over his body and machines that looked to do everything except make coffee. He had a central line in his neck and an NG tube up his nose. I knew from experience they were not comfortable. He was probably very thirsty and all they'll let him have are some ice chips.

I moved closer to his right side where I thought he would see me better. "Elliot? Babe? Can you hear me?"

He turned towards the sound of my voice, and I was able to see more of his mouth. He smiled at me, and I saw a sparkle in his beautiful hazel eyes.

"Hi there," he rasped. "Guess I did it this time, huh?"

"Babe don't worry about anything. The doctors here are the best this side of the Mississippi and they'll have you up and about in no time."

"Our house, our wedding, all plans. I'm so sorry, Henry," Elliot sobbed. The tears evident in his bandaging.

I rushed to his side and took his hand, the one without the strapping. I caressed his fingers and kissed his palm and then each finger. "Please don't worry about our plans. You keep dreaming about our life together. I want you to visualize the house you see us growing old in. I'll take care of the wedding arrangements, oh don't worry, I'll have Robin doing most of the creative part."

"Sounds good, but what if I, ah, what if my face is, is."

"Is what? You think I wouldn't marry you cuz of some scars on your face? Elliot Scott, shame on you. I would love you if you looked like the dog faced boy in the circus, or King Kong, or The Blob," I said with lots of hand gestures.

"Okay, I got it," Elliot said with a slight smile. "Getting tired, now. Gonna sleep. You be here when I wake up?"

"Nowhere else to be, my love. I'm going to call Robin and tell her about all of this."

"K, maybe she'll come here and keep you company. Are we far from home?"

"A ways. You're in Boulder City Hospital. The Clark County rescue got you out of your car. They are a great bunch of people."

"Hafta thank 'em. Night, Henry. Love you."

"Love you too, babe. See you soon."

I left the curtained area and Dr. Keys was waiting there with a couple of nurses.

"The nurses will prepare him for the operation. You and I can go to the conference room, and I'll break down for you what is going on with him. Do you need a few minutes?"

"Yeah, doc. I think I do. Can you direct me to the restrooms?"

"Down the hallway and turn left. You'll see them on your right. I'll be around here when you're ready."

I booked it down the hall and barely made it into a stall before my stomach came up to meet my tonsils. Mostly phlegm, as I hadn't eaten much today, but was still annoying. I flushed and sat down on the toilet and cried like a baby. Oh, my poor, poor Elliot. Why did this happen now, right when everything was going so well.

I pulled myself together, washed my hands and splashed cold water on my face, dried off and went in search of the doctor.

"Dr. Keys, I'm ready now, thank you for giving me a few."

"I've been doing this for a very long time, son. I recognize the signs," he said with a smile.

Looking at him, I judged him to be in his mid- sixties, with his white hair and face dotted with wrinkles, but nothing really noticeable. He was sharp, on his toes, and wide awake. I couldn't ask for more than that.

He brought me into a large room with an oval table taking up much of the floor space. There was a huge TV or computer screen hung on the wall in front of the room. Dr. Keys had me sit down facing the screen. He then proceeded to give me folders with a lot of medical jargon. They all had Elliot's name on them but beyond that, I had no clue what they were about.

"If you'll look to the screen, Hunter, you'll see an x-ray of a leg. Right along this area, he used a mouse to point everything out, you'll see a break near the ankle bone, it goes straight across the bottom of the leg, see it?"

"Yes, I do. Those are two different bones, aren't they?"

"Right you are. The tibia and fibula and they are broken straight across. He may end up with problems from it, but that is something we will deal with if and when the time comes. Right now, we are going to correct the break with plates and screws, then cast it."

"Next slide. This is his left arm. His ulna and radius are both broken as you can see. He also has a bruise on his collarbone, presumably from the seatbelt."

We'd only gotten to his leg and arm, and I was already feeling overwhelmed. I guess the good doctor sensed it.

"Why don't we sit for a minute. Here have some water," he said as he jumped up to get me a cup from the cooler in the corner of the room.

"Thanks, and I'm okay Doc. Show me what else he's going to have to deal with, or rather, what we'll be dealing with."

"I like your attitude, Hunter. It will go a long way in speeding Elliot's recovery. He said you were a keeper. I believe he was right."

"He said that? Jeez, that's him."

"I do have one question, before we continue. Why does he call you Henry?"

"Oh, it's a kind of a nickname. It's a really long story, but yeah, it's what he calls me."

"Okay, we had to ask him a few questions to make sure he was referring to you."

"I never think about it, he's the only one that calls me that. Sorry about that."

"No need okay let's look at the CAT scan. It shows some internal bleeding. This is the main reason for the surgery today. We don't know exactly where the bleed is or how bad. The surgeons will go in, find the bleeding and stop it. Simple as that, hopefully. If time allows and he's handling the anesthesia alright, the specialists are standing by for his arm and leg."

"Sounds awfully scary, routing around inside of him, looking for bleeders. What if he bleeds too much? Do you need blood? You can have all of mine if I match. I don't even know his blood type."

"Do you know your own?"

"Yeah, I do. I was in the hospital myself a few months back. My blood type is A+."

"Well coincidence will have it, so is Elliot," Keys said after consulting a folder on the table. "If we need blood, you will be the first to be called."

The next slide is of Elliot's head. It got bounced around quite a bit in the collision. He has a pretty bad concussion we are keeping a monitor on along with two black eyes and a broken cheekbone. His nose was banged up and bleeding, but no permanent damage has been found. He may need reconstructive surgery in the cheek area."

"I know of a great surgeon for that. Her name is Dr. Rachel Jewett, and she reconstructed my orbital area. Looks pretty good, huh?" I ran my fingers around my eye socket.

"I thought I detected some work done there. I know Rachel and she is the best. We will definitely call on her if we need to. So, now you have a clear picture of everything he's going to face in the next few months. None of his injuries are quick healing. He may be here with us for up to four months, and then to a rehab facility."

"It doesn't matter how long it takes, as long as he is healthy and pain free when it's all over. I can't stand for him to be in pain. Have you found out what caused the accident?"

"I've heard bits and pieces from the police. Apparently, someone going way too fast, lost control and went across the median and crashed into Elliot head on at top speed. He says he doesn't remember it and I think it may come back, but in small chunks that he can come to terms with easily."

"Oh my God. Hit head on, he must have been scared out of his mind when he saw it coming at him. I saw the tarp on the street, the other driver, I assume?"

"Yes, he was DOA, nothing could have brought him back. I don't believe he was wearing a seat belt, either."

"Thank goodness Elliot always buckles up and so do I."

"Hunter, stay here as long as you like. Go over any and all of the files, look at the slides again. Anything you want. I will come get you when he's in recovery and give you an update."

"Thank you, again, Dr. Keys. I'm going to call a good friend to both of us and let her know what's going on. She's waiting in LA for us to show up at her place. She may even insist on coming out here after I give her the news."

"We're here to help in any way possible. Let us know if you need something, anything."

"Thanks, doc. You have an incredible staff here."

"Yes, they are. Elliot couldn't be in safer hands; we're concerned with the whole person, not just the injuries. I'll be back to check on you."

After he left, I pulled my phone out, blew out a deep breath and pressed #2 on my speed dial.

"Hello, Hunter. Don't tell me you guys decided to stay over on the way back."

"Yeah but, um, Robin?" I cried into the phone.

"What's wrong? What happened? Is Elliot okay? Are you?"

So many questions being flung at me. "I'm fine, but Elliot's hurt. Bad, Robin."

"How did he get hurt?"

"Head on collision. The other driver he was, DOA. Apparently, he jumped the median and drove straight at Elliot. I've only briefly spoken to him, and I decided not to ask a lot of questions."

"Of course. How bad is it?"

"Broken leg, arm, may need reconstruction on his cheekbone and internal bleeding. He's in surgery now for that. They don't know where he's bleeding from or how bad.

Robin, I'm scared. What if he bleeds out? What if-"

"Stop that! Playing What If won't help either of you. Where are you?"

"Boulder City Hospital, Clark County right outside Las Vegas."

"Great, got it. I'll be there in a matter of hours. Okay for me to let Jim know?"

"Yes, please tell him."

"And our editor?"

"Yeah, him too. I'll talk to him, but not right now."

"Stay strong. I'll be there as soon as I can."

"Be safe, Robin. I mean it. Don't fuckin' get killed on me."

"I will, I promise. Love you. Talk soon."

"Same here."

Chapter Sixteen
Fast Changes, Slow Recovery

I had no more than hung up with Robin, than Dr. Keys walked through the door.

"Hunter? Elliot made it through surgery. The doctors found the bleeder and fixed it. He doesn't have a spleen anymore, but it really isn't necessary."

"Yes, I know. I don't have my spleen either."

"That hospital stay you mentioned?"

"Right. How soon can I see him?"

"Come with me. You should be able to see him when we get there. Remember, only a moment. He needs sleep more than anything else right now, except maybe seeing your face."

"Understood, doc. I'll put on my cheery face once we get there."

"Here we are," Dr. Keys said as we approached a large room with quite a few beds. Elliot was all the way in a corner. I got my happy face and smiled till my jaw hurt.

"Elliot? Hey you in there?"

"Mm, Henry?"

"Hi. The operation went well. Now you need to sleep. I'll see you in a little bit."

"K. Love you," Elliot whispered.

"Love you too," I replied. I bent down and kissed him on the forehead. He smiled as he drifted off to sleep.

"We'll watch him here in recovery for a while longer, then send him back to his room. You are welcome to stay down here or go up to his room, but whatever you decide, sleep has to be in the equation. You're dog tired, son. You need to rest."

"I am starting to feel it. Okay, I'll go up to his room and rest for a while."

Somewhere in the back of my head I heard voices. Mumbling scraps of language, though I could barely hear them. Next I heard "I don't really want to wake him. Looks like he was exhausted." Then I knew. Robin was here. I forced myself to become coherent and opened my eyes. Seeing her after all that's happened was too much for me. I sprang from the chair and threw myself into her arms. She eased me down to the empty bed and held and rocked me while I cried it all out. I was finally able to sit up and take a good look at her.

"I'm so glad you're here. You've been crying too," I said as I stroked her tear-stained cheek.

"You caught me, yeah I cried most of the way here. I went by what I believe was the accident scene. Nasty, I don't know how you kept it together. Is Elliot coming in here soon?"

Glancing at my watch, I became alarmed. It was almost an hour since Dr. Keys said he'd be coming shortly. Did something happen?

"Yes, let's find the doctor and see what the holdup is. First though, are you okay?" I said as I took her by the shoulders and looked straight into her eyes.

"I'm much better now that I'm here. Oh, I told Mr. Flanders the whole story and he said stay as long as you need to, and he expects a fine human-interest story when you get back."

"What a guy. I feel very guilty for deceiving him like I did," shaking my head, "Gotta learn to be more upfront and honest. Let's go find Elliot."

I took Robin by the hand and practically dragged her to the nurses station. I saw a nurse at the end of the enclosure and made a beeline towards her.

"Excuse me. Could you please tell me when Elliot Scott will be brought to his room?"

"I'm sorry but I'm not allowed to discuss the patients."

"But it's alright. I'm his fiancé and he's given permission for me to know about his condition. Ask Dr. Keys."

"Dr. Keys is a busy man. He's down in recovery helping out a patient. You are not allowed in there."

"You wanna bet? C'mon, Robin," I said as we quickly got on the nearest elevator.

"Wow. Did not like her at all," Robin quipped.

"Me either. The nurses down in the ER have all been so nice. Let's go find Dr. Keys. You'll be impressed with him."

We quickly made it down to the ER and I sought out the good doctor. I spotted him coming from a cubicle and rushed towards him.

"Dr. Keys!" I yelled in my whisper voice.

"Hunter, this must be the wonderful friend you were telling me about."

"Yes, Doc, this is Robin Hill, Robin, this is Dr. Keys, miracle worker extraordinaire."

"It's an honor to meet you, doctor. Hunter has been telling all you have done for our Elliot."

"It's a pleasure to meet you, Robin. I see you're quite the heroine yourself. Anyone that can calm this one down must be," Dr. Keys replied hooking his thumb towards Hunter.

"Doc, the nurse in recovery wouldn't tell me anything. She also told me not to bother you, as you were too busy to talk to me. Elliot is still there, and it's been hours. Can you find out why?"

"Of course, let's go right now. Betsy, I'm going to recovery. Be back shortly," the doctor told one of the nurses at the desk.

"Very good, doctor. Give Mr. Scott my best, she said with a smile.

"Will do, let's go you two," Doc said while half running down the corridor to the elevator.

Still holding Robin's hand, we followed onto the steel box that always felt to me to be swallowing its occupants.

"We'll get to the bottom of this, don't you worry now," the doctor said as the doors opened.

"That's her over there," I pointed to the stern looking nurse with the tight bun.

"Oh, that explains it. She scares me too," Dr. Keys whispered to us.

"Isobel," he called.

"Yes, Dr. Keys."

"Isobel, this is Mr. Wilson. He is Mr. Scott's fiancé. He is to be allowed in to see Mr. Scott whenever he wishes. Is that understood?"

"Y - Yes, sir. I wasn't informed of this gentleman's agreement."

"Maybe you should find out first. Would save a lot of time, don't you think?"

" I, ah, yeah, yes doctor."

"Now, Mr. Scott is still in recovery, why?"

"I don't really know. You can take it up with the doctor on duty."

"Hunter, Robin, let's go see what the problem is," Doc motioned for us to follow him.

I looked back at Nurse Isobel Vale. She had daggers shooting from her dark, cold eyes. She gave me the willies.

I saw Elliot in the same spot as earlier. He was sleeping and looked somewhat better, but with his face all bandaged it was hard to tell.

Dr. Keys went straight to a man in a white lab coat. They exchanged a few words with gestures towards Robin and I and Elliot.

It was pure torture for me to have to stay back. Good thing Robin was here. She sensed my anxiety and wrapped her arm around me and squeezed.

"He'll be fine. Probably just a precaution," Robin observed.

"Mm," was all I could manage.

Doctor Keys finally came over to us with a smile." I was beginning to love this man.

"It's okay. Elliot had some blood in his drainage tube. They were unsure of it and decided to keep him here under close observation. Hunter, Robin this is Dr. Chow. He's in charge of the recovery unit today. David, this is Elliot's fiancé, Hunter Wilson, and their best friend, Robin Hill."

Pleasantries exchanged, Dr. Chow said, "Why don't you spend a minute with Elliot. He's been in and out and also showing signs of having nightmares. I apologize too Mr. Wilson. I had no idea you were here."

"Not your fault, Dr. Chow. If Elliot asks for Henry, that's me."

"Yes, he has. Thanks, we had no clue who that was. We're going to keep him an hour or so longer, so we can rule out another bleed. Then back to his room he goes."

"Please, do whatever is best for him."

I shook hands with the doctor and headed for Elliot. Looking back, Robin was standing still. "Come on, girl. Let's see our boy," I said.

"Coming," Robin replied with a face of sunshine.

Approaching him quietly, I bent down and whispered, "Hey, sleepy head. Look who's here."

Eyes fluttering, Elliot opened them and smiled weakly at me. I gestured next to me, then guided Robin to the head of the bed.

"R - Robin? You came all this way? Thank you. Sorry, sleepy," Elliot yawned to prove his point.

"Ahh, we'll have plenty of time to talk. You sleep now," Robin bent down to kiss his cheek and squeeze his right hand. Smiling, he was out, again.

"Thank you so much, Dr. Keys. I feel so much better actually seeing him," I turned as we were walking out. I swear I heard Nurse Vale growl.

"You are both welcome to go and stay up in his room to wait for him. I've got to get back down to the ER, but you know where you're going, right?"

"Sure do and thanks again," I said.

Doc waved to us from the elevator and disappeared like a magician's assistant in a magic show.

Robin and I went the other way to go back to Elliot's room. After we got halfway to it, my stomach growled, loudly!

"Hunt, when did you eat last?"

"Um, sometime before we left Vegas, I think."

"Cafeteria first, then Elliot's room, deal?" Robin challenged.

Another loud noise from my tattletale stomach and I agreed. "But only a few minutes then we go, K?"

"As long as you eat something," Robin said as she led me to the large open room.

"I really don't know what I want. I'm not too hungry."

"I'll get something light for you. Go get us a table."

"Yes ma'am. Right away, ma'am," I barked with a mock salute.

"Oh, shush now. Go sit down," she said as her face turned bright red from the teasing.

"I found a quiet table near a bank of windows and took a seat. Robin arrived within minutes with a tray full. I helped her settle it on the table and she began to dole out the contents.

"Here you go, some nice hot tomato soup. Here are the crackers and this is a grilled cheese sandwich she explained before letting me have the plate. She had a Caesar salad with grilled chicken. I took a spoonful of the thick, flavorful soup and that was that; I practically drank the bowl right down. I ate the sandwich with about as much gusto.

"Jeez, Hunter, you almost inhaled all of it. Too bad you weren't hungry."

"I know, right? Guess I was," I said sheepishly. "I feel a lot better now, though."

"I'm glad. You had me worried. I was afraid you might pass out from hunger."

"No, doing better. I'm going to slowly stretch out my legs. They're the ones that give me trouble if and when we get up. Too many worms in my legs. Too much sitting around for me. The restlessness is bringing on the pain. I'll be fine with some stretching and with my belly full I can think clearly."

"Good, then I'm gonna call Joe and give him an update," Robin volunteered.

"Thanks for taking care of that. I'll call Mr. Flanders and let him know what's going on."

"Sounds good. I'll call from outside. You stay here with your feet up."

I settled down into the chair, picked up the phone and dialed the number.

"Yeah, Flanders, here."

"Mr. Flanders, it's Wilson."

"Oh, jeez Wilson. How are you doing?"

"Okay, sorry I haven't called until now."

"Understandable, my boy. How is your friend? Robin indicated he was quite badly hurt."

"Yes, he is and he's not just a friend, sir. We're getting married."

"Oh, I see. Well, congratulations to both of you."

"This was the story I went after."

"Yes, and by the sounds, I'd say you've got a great human-interest piece starting there. Can't wait for the ending."

"Me either," I said softly.

"You take your time getting back, we can say it's research. Robin too."

"Thank you, Mr. Flanders. We both appreciate your understanding."

"Nonsense. Makes perfect sense from my standpoint. I get a great story for my paper, and haven't I been married to the love of my life for forty-three years? Yes, I have so I do understand, young man."

I saw Robin coming with my peripheral vision and said goodbye to Mr. Flanders and hung up. I was pleased and amazed how well it went.

"Hey, Joe says Hi. I think I could've convinced him to come, but he really is swamped at the station."

"That's okay. I don't expect people to drop their lives and run out here. Nobody like you around, Robin."

Right then and there at that moment Robin burst into tears and I grabbed her, held her and talked in whispers to assure her we would all be Jim dandy, Elliot too.

She was calming down when they brought Elliot's bed around the corner. He was still sleeping, but his color was good.

Doctor Chow brought up the rear of the procession line, looking pleased with himself.

“Hey, Doc. How is he?”

“He’s doing excellent, Hunter. After a couple of days, we will assess the arm and the leg breaks. We have him in soft casts right now, but that can’t continue for very long.”

“He was too weak to do it the first time around, I gather,” added Robin.

“That’s correct. Oh, Ms. Hill, we gained permission from Elliot to discuss his medical conditions with you as well as Mr. Wilson, so feel free to ask anything you care to.”

"Thank you. I was concerned about the breaks because, Hunter here, he broke his leg with the same two bones, and I remember the doctors being very concerned about it. He also had internal injuries and lost his spleen, just like Elliot. You know it's rather spooky how you both ended up with about the same injuries," Robin reveled.

"Mr. Wilson, Hunter, when did this occur? I do see a small scar where you've had reconstructive surgery on your orbital area, but other than that, I'd never have known. Do you mind me asking, was it Rachel Jewett that performed your surgery?"

"Yes, it was. It's amazing how all of you docs seem to know each other's handiwork. I know Dr. Jewett is a gifted surgeon, so you and Dr. Keys knowing her, makes me feel pretty good. I already talked to Dr. Keys about getting her if Elliot needs his cheekbone replaced. She's on his list if and when he needs it."

"I suppose most surgeons are artists and each one has their own unique style. Yes, Rachel is extremely gifted, she studied under me," the good doctor said with a laugh.

"That's also good to hear. So, you figure he's gonna sleep through the night, now?"

"Yes, and no. He will sleep until some mean nurse comes in to give him meds, check his vitals, take blood, monitor his draining and feeding tubes and a host of other reasons to bother the poor sick people in here."

"Oh, I remember those days. I was glad to go home so I could get some rest. But I also understand how important it is."

"I'll leave you now. I will be back in a couple of hours to check on him. The chairs in the room are very comfy and lay almost flat so you can sleep. I ordered some blankets and pillows to be brought in for you both. As long as you let him sleep, I have no problem with you staying in the room with him."

"Don't worry, Dr. Chow. We won't disturb him at all, right Robin?"

"Absolutely. We both know just how important rest is."

"Very well, I will see you later. Anything you need, please don't hesitate to ask."

"Thank you for everything, doc. You and Dr. Keys are the best."

After he left, I went over to get a better look at my soulmate. He looked so young, like a child. I still couldn't really see his face, but I noticed they did take some of the bandaging off. Elliot had a chunk of skin gone from along his jawline. I wondered how bad the rest of his face was. I couldn't give a shit if he had scars, but being an actor, his face was his business card. He made a living from his body, and if that was damaged, I wondered how he would handle it.

"Hunt?" Robin murmured in my ear. She wrapped her two arms around my right arm and laid her head on my shoulder.

"You okay?" she inquired.

"Yeah, just thinking. Let's go across the room and talk," I said as I bent to kiss Elliot's forehead. I was impressed with the coolness of it.

Robin and I settled into the two overstuffed lounge chairs and talked softly. As usual, Robin was reading my mind.

"Don't tell me, you're wondering how Elliot will react upon finding out his face was damaged in the crash, right?"

"Man, girl. Spot on," I said in awe.

"I think he'll have a tough time, at first, but after many ego boosting sessions with you and me, he'll get over it. Plus, I'm sure plastic surgery will be possible, after he heals, of course."

"Thanks for making it so simple. It's a complicated mess, but I will focus on the end result and that should help to get him through it. If we're not enough, there are professionals he can go see. My biggest fear is that if there is much damage, he will postpone or, heaven forbid, call off the wedding."

"Never."

I jerked my head up quickly. That came from the other side of the room. Out of the chair I bounded too fast and almost fell on my ass. I got to Elliot just as his eyes were closing.

"Elliot, did you say, Never?"

"Yeah," he replied, keeping his eyes closed. "Never call off the wedding. You said you didn't care what I looked like, so you get me as I am."

"I meant it, babe. I don't care if you look like Frankenstein's monster under all that gauze, I love you for you, not cause you're pretty."

"That goes for me too, I am still maid of honor/best man at this shindig, and I really want a wedding to plan."

"You go for it, sweet Robin. Such a good friend. Take care of Henry while I'm stuck in here. He won't even eat if you don't watch him. Goin' ta sleep now. Night."

"Elliot's got your number, huh?" Robin teased.

"Yeah, so he was right about the eating part. Oh, stop gloating, missy."

The days jumbled into the nurses schedules, and I only knew what time it was by the nurse and what she or he was visiting for. They came in every couple of hours for something or other. Elliot had both his leg and his arm set in the same session. Apparently, they had both the arm and leg specialists working on him at the same time. He now sported casts on both sides of his body and not too happy about it. Me, I was thrilled that he was well enough to complain. The docs all say he's making a rapid recovery and it shows.

Most of the IV's, including the central line, had been removed and he was looking much more human. They are going to remove the feeding tube next and try him on human food.

"Thank goodness for that. I'm lying here starving and they won't bring me a damn thing to eat," Elliot groused.

“They can’t, babe. You’re still using the feeding tube.”

“Oh, like that’s filling me up. Yeah, okay. Sorry, I’m a grouch.”

“You have every right to be pissy. I remember what it was like being tied down to a hospital bed twenty-four/ seven. It sucks petunias.”

“Sucks petunias?” Elliot smirked, then giggled and then gave an all-out belly laugh that unfortunately led to having to call the nurse as he laughed himself into a hurting unit. But, boy, did it feel good to see my Elliot lurking right inside of the fake one.

“Ow, oh thanks Nurse Daniels. I guess I laughed too hard. Man, that hurts, but it felt really good, for a few minutes.

“I’m sorry, babe. It was my fault for making you laugh,” I chided myself.

“No, honest, babe, it felt wonderful, until it didn’t,” Elliot smiled again. They’d removed much more of the bandages and the scars were fairly evident. He hadn’t asked for a mirror, and I wasn’t about to suggest it. That dimple, though, it was still prominent on his cheek, and I fell in love with him all over again every time I looked at him.

“If you two can’t behave, I’ll have to separate you,” Nurse Daniels reprimanded, but with a twinkle in her eyes.

Robin walked in at that moment. She must have overheard the nurse as her first words were, “What have you two been up to? I can't leave here for five minutes without you getting into some kind of trouble."

"We weren't doing anything, honest," I replied.

"It was all his fault," Elliot ratted on me.

"Oh, I've no doubt he was involved, but I think you were just as much to blame, Elliot Scott," Robin tried to say with a straight face, but didn't quite make it.

"Seriously, are you alright, Elliot? Nurse Daniels just gave you a pain shot," she said very concerned.

"Yeah, Henry said something that struck me funny, and I laughed too hard. I'm okay. I'm so frustrated that I can't even laugh out loud without causing some kind of bother to everybody," Elliot said dejected.

"I totally get it, babe. I was in the same boat as you are not so long ago. I'm not gonna give you sappy platitudes or say it'll get better, just be patient. That one used to drive me straight up the wall! It sucks, plain and simple and there's not a damn thing any of us can do to change it. You're getting healthier and stronger every day, and I know you don't believe that either, but it's true."

"Hunt's right, Elliot. I even see the transformation in you. Hey, you're well enough to bitch about everything, I'd say that was progress," Robin added.

"I'd have to agree with that statement myself," Dr. Keys said as he strolled into the room.

"Hey, Doc. What's it time for now? More blood? Need to prick my finger for sugar? Checking on my output? Maybe my input? I'm all yours," Elliot said snarly.

"I'm actually checking on your input right now. I think we can remove the tube and get you eating regular food. Big day, huh?" the doctor quipped.

"Oh, okay, Doc. I deserve that, sorry. Please don't make me laugh again, it hurts too much. I really am appreciative of everything everyone has been doing for me, it's just sometimes-"

"Sometimes you'd like to jump out of bed and go take a piss all by yourself, right?" Dr. Keys said with a dead pan face.

"Yes, yes, that's it exactly, you nailed it doc. And Henry, I'm sorry if I ever made you feel useless or worse about yourself when you were laid up. I honestly had no idea until now."

"Elliot, you could never have made me feel bad in that way. You were always a ray of sunshine to brighten my otherwise dreary days. You and Robin, my saviors."

"I feel that way about you guys, too." Elliot answered as the doctor was poking around his stomach. A nurse breezed in with a small kit of some sort. She took little tools from it and handed them to the doctor. Of course, they were both wearing gloves.

"Are you taking the thing out right now?"

"Oh, yeah. It's just a few snips and out it comes." While he was talking, he and the nurse successfully removed the feeding tube from the young actor's stomach. A large piece of gauze with an antibiotic was taped in the tubes place.

"We're bringing you a tray shortly. Only bland foods right now, some broth, cream of wheat, yogurt, and if you're a really good boy, ice cream for dessert," Dr. Keys teased.

"Oh, for ice cream I'll be extra good, doc. Promise," Elliot said with his arm raised to the oath.

The entire room quieted down as we all watched the doorway expectantly. Every squeak must surely be his first meal. It was about ten minutes later the tray finally showed up. Doc Keys had been paged to an emergency and had left by this time. The kitchen helper girl brought the large tray, placed it on the small wheeled table then brought the whole thing over to Elliot. She took the cover off of the tray and Robin and I crowded around to see what delicacies he'd been given.

"Oh, boy look at all of this," he observed. "It's exactly what Dr. Keys said. There's broth, and it smells of chicken. I like that. I'm not crazy about Cream of Wheat, however."

"It's okay, babe. They give you a variety of foods that you're allowed so you can pick and choose what you like. You'll start filling out menus now. Then you can get what you want, well, within reason. I never ate the Cream of Wheat either."

"Good, so we won't have any in our home, right?" Elliot looked up at me with those innocent eyes.

"No, none in our home," I said as tears threaten to roll from my eyes.

"What's wrong, Henry? Did I say something wrong?"

Barely able to answer him, I whispered, "No, you said everything just right. It's just so comforting for you to talk about an us in your future. You hadn't said anything, and I was getting nervous you'd changed your mind."

"C'mere, babe," Elliot twisted his body to the side. As I approached, he put his right arm out straight and used the casted arm as best he could. He wrapped his arms around me, and I felt so loved and safe, I let the tears fall.

"I love you so much, Elliot. I can't wait until we can make plans in earnest."

"Why can't you do that now?" Robin piped up.

"Huh? What do you mean, little girl?" I asked with a furrowed brow.

"Why can't you guys at least start looking for a place to live? We have WIFI in here and one of us has always got a laptop or a tablet floating around. Start looking up where you wanna live and check out houses in those areas. It's not rocket science, ya know."

Elliot and I stared at her for a long moment and then in unison replied, "Yeah, why not?"

"Good, here's one tablet on the windowsill. Go to it. I'm gonna go down to the cafeteria and get a salad or maybe cheat off my diet and get a cheeseburger. You boys have a good time, and no trouble making while I'm gone."

"Now why didn't we think of that?" I mused.

"I don't know, I guess some things take a woman's brain."

"You need to eat something here, so I'll look up places first, you just tell me where you wanna live."

"Alright, I'll drink this broth first. It smells really good." Elliot said as he took a sip.

"Well, how is it?"

"It's actually pretty good, but I can tell, even from the first sip, I won't be eating much. I think I'll have the ice cream now, so I'll have room for dessert."

"That's smart thinking," I said. I was elated Elliot was beginning to feel happy. Our Robin was a true angel.

"You had mentioned living by the ocean and I like that idea too," Elliot said with a mouth full of vanilla ice cream.

"Okay, let's see what availability there is along the ocean line. We have to think in terms of you getting to the studios. You don't want to have a long commute."

"I don't think we need to worry about that. I doubt anyone will hire me after getting a look at my face."

I froze. This was the first time he'd mentioned his face. How much did he know? How bad was it? I didn't even know. I had to be optimistic for him. As I turned to face him, I made sure my smile was screwed on tightly.

"Elliot, you don't know how much damage there is to your face. And even if there is more than you'd like, there is always plastic surgery.

"I know but my face is worse than Frankenstein's monster."

"How would you know that?" I asked, fearing the answer.

"How do ya think? I peeked."

"When was this?"

"A few days ago. You and Robin were sleeping, and the nurse had left the metal tray that holds the meds. Makes a great mirror."

"Alright, you're a step ahead of me, since I haven't seen it, but I still say, you are recovering from the surgeries. Your body is dealing with all of that. Once you're pretty well healed, then your system can concentrate on your face. I think you'll see a vast improvement rather quickly."

"That's bullshit, Henry, and I love you for thinking it all up, " Elliot smiled.

"It's not all bullshit. I've read articles about the body's healing powers, but it can only handle so much at once. I swear, Elliot, I'm not lying," I said and almost heard the 'for once' after my statement.

"I believe you, babe. It does make sense. But my thought was to get a place closer to your paper. You go to one place every day. I get tossed around to different studios. Better to be stable for you."

"Elliot Scott, you are the most selfless person on the planet. I love you so much it hurts."

"I don't want you hurting, but I love you that much, too. Mm, that ice cream was good."

"I'm glad, now try the yogurt. It's orange cream, sounds good."

While Elliot was wrestling with the yogurt wrapping, I checked beach front properties closer to my work.

"Um, I think it's gonna be too expensive for us to live there," I said, flipping through the listings. " The houses start at a million and increase in price from there."

"What's the problem? You don't like any of them?" Elliot asked around a mouthful of yogurt.

"Ah, no, it's the million-dollar price tag I have an issue with."

"Is that all?"

"Is that all?" I repeated, a bit snarky. " Where do you think we're going to get that kind of money? Blow it out the ass?"

"No, but I could take it from one of several bank accounts, or we can use the money from the sale of my house."

"Wait, what? You have bank accounts, as in plural, with over a million dollars in them? And your house, that's worth that much?"

"Yeah, but to be accurate I would imagine that two of the accounts have closer to two and a half million, could be three now, with interest. And as for my house, I could probably easily get eleven million for it."

"Eleven, eleven, mill- mill-"

"Spit it out, Henry, you can do it," Elliot teased.

"I'm glad you're having so much fun. You know what I'm worth? I got eight thousand, two hundred, sixty-three dollars and twenty-eight cents to my name, and that's only cuz I've scrimped and saved. That Vegas money was a real windfall to me."

"I'm sorry, sweetheart. I don't mean to be flip, it's just somethin I've always had. I live in the house my parents bought. It belonged to Mary Tyler Moore, so how much do you think it sold for? And as for your worth, I don't judge a person's worth by their bank account. You are priceless to me, and don't you forget that" Elliot said tenderly.

"Thanks for that, and I guess I never thought about it cuz your so down to earth. You drive a fancy car but that's about status. You've never made me feel like the poor kid from the wrong side of the tracks."

"Okay, so we can look at some of those properties without getting all freaked out about price, right?" Elliot cocked his head towards me.

"Yes, we can." I sat on the bed with him and showed him the homes I'd seen for a million six up to eight million. There was one I really liked for two and a half million. It had a wraparound farmer's porch and a foyer with a fourteen-foot ceiling. Perfect for the Christmas tree. Large galley kitchen fully equipped, huge family room with fireplace. Good sized den off the foyer. Three bedrooms and full bath upstairs, half bath downstairs next to the laundry room. The exterior was cream colored with evergreen trim.

Elliot skimmed through the pictures, stopped, went back and spent some time looking at something. He finally looked up, smiled, and said, "I like this one."

Taking the tablet, I already knew. It was the house I loved. I looked down and back up at him, smiling ear to ear.

"You like it, too, Henry?"

"Yes, I love it," I said softly.

"Yeah, I think it's perfect. Wanna hand me my phone?"

"Sure."

Elliot dialed and started a conversation. "Hey, Betty, Elliot Scott. Listen, I'm gonna be selling that ole rat trap of mine. You want the listing? Great, you've got a house at 24759 (fill in) Hwy. selling for two and a half mill. I want it. What? Yes, I'm serious. I'm getting married and my fiancé and I want to live in that house. Yeah, no foolin'. Yes, well thank you. Now I'm kind of, um, tied up at the moment and can't get over there. I'll send Sid's team over to clean my house from top to bottom for you, but listen, Betty. I want that oceanfront property, today if possible, okay? Your welcome, and thanks to you. Call me when the deal is done. Bye."

"And that my dear, Henry is how it's done."

I was amazed, shocked, captivated. I couldn't believe with one phone call Elliot got us that beautiful home.

"I'm speechless. You're amazing."

"Eh, it's all in who you know. Now, I gotta call Sid to get his team over to my house."

As he was waiting to connect, he said, "You know that foyer would be the perfect place for a Christmas tree."

That did it, I leaned over and gave him a good Ole Fashioned French kiss.

"Hey, Sid, Elliot Scott here," he said while laughing into the phone.

"Hello, Mr. Scott. What can I do for you?"

"Need you to clean my house, top to bottom. I'm selling her so I need a thorough job, naturally I thought of you. No, I won't be there, but I'll put a deposit into your account. I'll talk it over with my fiancé and let you know. Alright, bye and thanks."

"What will you talk over?" I asked.

"Oh, he wants to know if he will be hired to clean our new place."

"Sure, I mean, you know him and trust him, so it's alright with me. Cleaning has never had a great appeal to me."

"He is a good guy, and his team is great. I'll let him know when I deposit his fee."

"I'm back, guys. What's up?" Robin asked as she glided into the room.

"You wanna tell her?" I asked.

"Here, show her the picture."

"This is our new home, " I said as I handed Robin the tablet.

"Wow, this is gorgeous, love the colors. So, you got any more apple pie dreams?"

"It is a dream, but a dream come true," I said.

"What are you talking about? You been taking Elliot's pain meds or something?"

"Really, Robin. Elliot called the real estate agent, who he happens to know, and told her she could have the listing of his house if she bought this one," I gestured to the screen.

"Unbelievable, that's so crazy. I'm speechless," Robin rambled.

"That's what I said too."

"He got over it quick enough, "Elliot retorted.

"You gonna get married on the beach at the house?"

"Yes, or inside the house. There's a very pretty den with a fireplace that would make a nice ceremony venue," Elliot offered.

"Elliot's right, excellent idea, babe."

"This is getting exciting. I wanna help, what can I do? Robin asked.

"Not much we can do from here, right now. Maybe you could work on the color schemes, menus and decorations," Elliot suggested after seeing her face fall with disappointment.

"Oh, I would love that. May I see the tablet.? Yes, here it is, the den. It's a colonial blue, like a peacock blue. We could go with lighter shades of blue and maybe yellow accents."

"Sounds nice. Henry and I could do the blue ties and pocket handkerchiefs and a yellow lapel flower."

"Now, that's what I'm talking about!" Robin exclaimed. "I'm thinking the dining room here would be fine for the reception. I'm not wrong in assuming it will be small and intimate, am I?"

"No, you're correct, a small gathering," I confirmed.

"Joe," Elliot added.

"Yes, of course we'll invite Joe," but Elliot was looking past me. Then Joe saddled up alongside me.

"Oh, you meant Joe's here," I laughed.

"Hey guys, sorry it took me so long to get here. Couldn't get away from my desk. Hunter how's it going?"

"It's going, Joe. We're making wedding plans."

"Wow, really? I'm truly happy for you both. I'm invited, right?"

"Yes, of course, Joe." Elliot stated.

Joe stood up against Elliot's bed and put a hand on his shoulder. "How are you doing, son?"

"Much better since our genius angel over there thought of making wedding plans. And here's our new home," Elliot said showing Joe the pictures. "Babe, it's official. I got a text from Betty. Bought house for you, text me the fax number where you are to sign the papers.

"It's really our place?"

"All ours."

"Looks like I showed up at the right time."

"Joe, you have no idea how great this is. How you feeling, babe," I asked quietly.

"I'm feeling like everything is going to work out," Elliot looked at me with such love in his eyes. " I don't know how, but I'm gaining confidence."

We both looked over at Robin and I said, "You, c'mere you," I grabbed her and spun her around the room until we were dizzy. We all yelled and laughed and just had fun.

Happy and content. For the first time in a long time, and it felt wonderful.

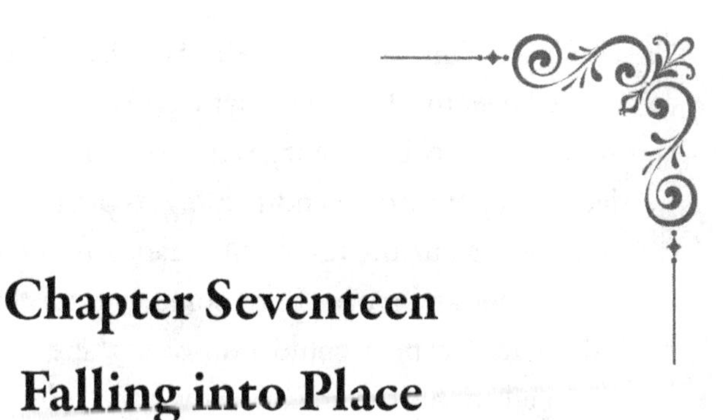

Chapter Seventeen
Falling into Place

We were all happy that afternoon. Then my reality overshadowed my positive thoughts and brought me back down again. Especially now, in that special hour in the night when the sky, moon, and stars all seem their sharpest.

I get so angry here in this bed, watching my life flutter in front of my eyes and not being an active participant.

I get angry and scared. Oh, so scared, of myself, mainly, but of Henry too. Scared he's gonna decide an ugly husband is out of the question. Then I berate myself for even thinking Henry could ever be that shallow.

My thoughts twist and turn then go up and down like two evenly matched kids on a teeter-totter.

Then with one suggestion from our earthly angel, Robin, my world flip-flopped backed to rightness once again. I was happy for real, not faking it, but the genuine article. I thought for a minute or two of the proper definition of my thoughts and feelings. I looked over at Henry, sound asleep in the chair, covers pulled over his nose, looking like a two-bit bank robber on the late, late, late, show and it washed over me. Joy. I was joyful and going over today in my mind's eye, I think Henry was too. I'm looking forward to decorating our home and helping to plan our joyous event. That's what our invites should read, I thought, hm, I need some paper and a pen. I saw some over on the window sill. I thought maybe I could hop over there and get them. I managed to get the free foot over the side of the bed so I could balance easier. I lifted the casted one with my hands over the side. I just went to stand up when I heard-

"Elliot Scott? What the fuck are you trying to do?"

"I, ah, well, see, babe, I wanted that paper and pen over there. Thought I could reach from here."

Henry looked at me with such a stern face, I burst out laughing, which woke Robin.

"What's going on, partying without me?"

"Never, " I said.

Henry growled. "I'll get those things for you, but-"

"Yeah, I know, no jumping out of bed."

"What's so urgent you need them right now?

"I had an idea for our wedding invites and wanted to write a few thoughts down."

"Oh, I see, well that's a really good answer. Here you go," Henry said as he passed me the paper and pen.

I began to think of the cover. The cover of the card should read JOY and inside:

Join in our Joy and
Bask in the glow of our love
As Hunter Wilson and Elliot Scott become
Mr. & Mr. Hunter and Elliot Wilson-Scott

"What do ya think of this? I asked Henry.

"I think it's perfect, simply perfect. Your ideas are incredible and seem to always capture the true us."

"What did you say?" I stared right through him.

"About?"

"About when you read this, you said what, um, simply perfect. I love that. Our love is Simply Joy; this could be the cover.

"Oh, yes it's just right, babe. I was thinking, could we have a lemon cream cake?"

"You can have any kind of cake you want."

"Elliot, these ideas of yours, it's like you wrote what was in my head."

"I'm sure you could do better, after all, you're the writer in the family."

"No way. You've done an extraordinary job. If you and I could reproduce, we'd probably end up with a Pulitzer Prize winner."

"You'd be a great father, you know. Except," I trailed off.

"Except. men can't have babies."

"C'mere, Henry." I cooed to him with my good arm extended. He came to me with his eyes downcast and that was on me. I took him gently into my arm and he wrapped his arms around my back and slowly stroked it. I tried to reciprocate but didn't quite make it.

"I'm very sorry if I hurt your feelings. I know you're sensitive about this. I wouldn't hurt you for the world, honest."

"Let's make more wedding plans."

"I'm up for that!" I exclaimed with a huge grin.

"Me, too" Robin declared from across the room.

"Then get over here, girl. Let's plan."

We spent hours looking at flowers, decorations, centerpieces, favors, color schemes, cakes, and food.

"I was thinking about all of the plans and notes and all and I was wondering, uhm," Robin started.

"Wondering what? Speak up girl," Henry said.

"Should we be working on all of this before getting your house ready? I mean, we're talking about the ceremony in your den and the reception at the dining room table, guys, you don't have a dining room table," Robin said sheepishly.

Henry and I stopped talking and stared dumbly at her, then at each other. We began to giggle which led to a full-blown laughing session. We couldn't stop and laughed till we cried. Robin kept shaking her head as she frantically looked for a crockpot that matched the color scheme in the kitchen.

"How much stuff do you have to bring with you, Henry?"

"I would say, one trip with the smallest U-Haul should do it. I have very little and remember, I live there to watch over the place, nothing in it is mine. My personal stuff shouldn't take that much to move. Oh, well, there is one thing,"

"What is this one thing," I asked, intrigued.

"I have a favorite chair-"

"Oh no you don't mister," Robin said angrily. "You're not bringing that ugly thing to that beautiful new house."

"Okay, now I have to know, what's this thing look like?"

"It's not that bad, really. It's comfortable. It was my Dad's."

"It's not that it's horrible looking, not like Martin's chair on Frasier, but it's so out of date with today's stuff. It's green, like a dark green, heavy as hell, and when you push the seat back to lounge in it, sawdust flies out from underneath," Robin explained.

"Ha ha, it sounds like it has a personality of its own. I love it already!" I told them.

"Oh, you're impossible! Mark my words, you'll live to regret taking in that chair, Elliot."

"Never."

"What about your place, Elliot?" Henry inquired.

"That's deceiving, actually. Most of the furniture came with it. Along with all the pots and pans and whatever else one keeps in the kitchen. The bed is mine in my room and just my clothes and a few personal items, well I do have a closet that contains a bunch of boxes that belonged to my parents, but that's about it. My personal items in the bathroom and a little bit of food in the cupboards and fridge."

"Oh, yeah, I got a six-pack in my fridge too."

"So, you're planning a wedding in a house that has no furniture, and how long do you think you could keep that a secret?" Robin quipped.

"Maybe, " Henry and I chorused.

"Maybe, what?" asked Robin.

I yielded to Henry as I felt we were thinking the same thing.

"Maybe we shouldn't rush the wedding thing, I mean slow it down, just a bit, until we get the house fixed up to just the way we want it. We could have just as much fun and just as many fights over curtains and potato peelers as what flowers to have at the ceremony. I mean, as long as we're together, that's what's important, right?"

"To be honest, that's about what I was going to say, except for the potato peeler. We could hold off making wedding plans for a couple of months while I'm still healing and we can put together our dream home, yes?" I agreed.

"As much as I love doing the wedding plans, I really believe you're both thinking logically and reasonable. I have no problem switching from wedding planner to interior decorator, I wear many hats!" Robin said happily.

"What's wrong, babe," Henry asked, noticing Elliot pouting.

"I did all that laughing and didn't have to call 911, and neither of you even noticed!" Elliot whined, but with sparkling eyes.

"It's a miracle, babe. Actually, you're the miracle. You're making giant leaps in recovery. Doc Keys says it's cuz you have a naturally positive constitution."

"Huh, how about that." Telling him I was ready to give up many times didn't seem appropriate.

I finally feel like there might be some hope for me yet. Henry tries so hard to be chipper. No one can keep that up twenty-four seven, not even me.

Since the night I peeked under my bandages, I've not wanted to do anything. Of course, I do, but just so they won't know how low I've sunk. I've even been wondering how to get out of this wedding, short of suicide. I'm not that desperate, not yet anyway.

I feel I'm living in a damn three-ring circus. I'm the freak show, Henry's the crowd pleaser. Running around trying to keep me happy, and Robin. She's the glue holding the whole lot of us together, like the MC keeping account of all of us acts.

My face, oh God, my face. It's horrible. I make a living on my looks, what do I do now? I believe Henry when he says he still wants to marry me, and he was clueless about the money. He was also genuinely shocked about my house and the cash on hand. No, Henry has his faults, for one he's a habitual liar. He can't help himself. Probably something to do with his mom dying when he was so young. I'm responsible for him being a liar as well. It was my family that killed her. That makes me guilty as well.

Aside from the lying, Henry's one of the sweetest, most generous and thoughtful person I know. I love him to pieces but is it fair making him be saddled with me. We don't have the testing and reports back yet, and I try so not to look discouraged too much. If I find out my case is hopeless, I may opt for suicide then.

I was determined to get better and let my body heal. There was so much to be glad about, okay, Pollyanna I'm not, but having Henry and Robin here helped me to get out of the blue funk I'd been in, worrying about my stupid face. After a couple of therapy sessions with Hurricane Hilda and you weren't thinking how pretty you were or weren't. I buckled down and worked hard. Henry and Robin were with me every step of the way for the first two weeks. Then Robin told us she needed to get back home. Mr. Flanders, the editor of their paper, was understanding of Henry's staying but thought it best Robin go back to work.

On a particularly chilly, gray, drizzly morning, we said goodbye.

"Now, it's not good bye, guys, it's merely so long. I'll text and call so much you'll be hanging up on me."

"Yeah, right," Henry choked out.

"Hey, look at it this way, I can go to Elliot's place and see how it looks, and if it's moving on the market, go to Hunter's place and explain the situation and how you're going to be leaving, and then I can go to your new house and take oodles of pictures and send them off to you for furniture decisions."

"Well, that sounds very nice, but like a lot for you to take on," I said doubtfully.

"Now, look here, I'm a master task manipulator. Don't you worry about me," Robin glowed.

"Okay, it's alright with me, you mind her going to your house, Elliot?"

"Not in the least, and I'm dying to see pictures of our home. So, you have permissions all around. Thank you, sweet angel. We'll miss you but understand."

"We've been lucky to have had you here this long," Henry added.

A quick hug and kiss from both of us and out the door she fled.

"You alright, Henry?" I asked as soon as she was gone.

"Mm, yeah, I'm resisting the urge to run after her. I know she was crying."

"Yes, and so are we. It's hard, but we must learn to accept what we can't change."

"Well, listen to Mr. Philosophy over there," Henry grinned as he came to my side.

"I'm just trying to get out of here as fast as possible. If it means reciting a few platitudes, so be it."

Turned out, fast was ten weeks. Docs Keys and Chow didn't want me leaving until I was able to use both my arm and leg. I kept telling them I wouldn't be driving. My car was smashed up like a pancake. Henry would be doing all the driving, but they were adamant. They also got in touch with specialists in Los Angeles to take my case when I got back there.

The last piece of my recovery was of course, my face. The bandages were removed, and I insisted Henry leave the room. No sense scaring him to death immediately. I was handed a mirror and after several minutes of grasping it to my body, I somehow got the courage to actually look at myself. Holding my breath, I slowly raised the reflecting tool up enough to see. It really wasn't as bad as I'd dreamed it was. I thought I would walk around as Picasso's only breathing work of art. It wasn't pretty, though. I had scars where stitches had been across my forehead and down my left cheek. They managed to fix my cheekbone without reconstructive surgery, but the scars were there. Most were from chunks of glass from, well probably both cars. So, not quite Frankenstein's monster, but I was in no danger of being called Pretty Boy any time soon.

Dr Keys was with me the whole time watching.

"You know they do have ways to fix all that now."

"Fix all what, doc?"

"Your face," he said without so much as a smirk.

We both laughed. "Now can I get that fiancé of yours? The nurses tell me he's having kittens in the hallway."

"Ha Ha, sure let him come in. He's probably put a ditch in the floor with his pacing."

Henry was at my side in a flash. Eyes wide open and soft, he looked over every inch of my face. With his gentle hands on either side of my head, he began to kiss every scar on my face. The tears started to flow as I wondered what I possibly did to deserve this man.

"Elliot, it's really not too bad. I won't lie, I promise, you do have some scarring and a few along your forehead are deep. But I think any plastic surgeon will be able to help, and since we won't get you just anybody, only the best for you, I bet we will have to use a magnifying glass to see the scars when it's all healed."

"Thank you, babe. You always say the right thing."

Right then, Hilda flew in on her broom stick to take me to therapy. Since the casts had come off, two days prior, she worked me twice as hard at each session.

"So, they took off your bandages, eh?"

"Yeah, Hilda. What do you think of the new me?"

"Not much, but I didn't think much of the old you, either. Let's go."

As I got into the wheelchair she had rolled in, I said, "Be home soon love. Why don't you text Robin and see where we stand."

"Good idea, I will. Have fun at therapy, Sweet Pea."

Hilda, who didn't care much for homosexuals, but then again, she wasn't too keen on heterosexuals either, made a face and pushed me out the door, hard.

After a few more grueling sessions like that, the doctors finally agreed to let me leave. I'd been ambulatory for almost two weeks, no casts, no crutches. A little limping but otherwise I was good.

I forced myself to eat the slop they served me so the staff would get favorable reports from the dietary staff. Then I would beg Henry to sneak me in a cheeseburger. After I got caught with a few fries in my sheets, the doctors decided it was time to boot me out.

"Yes, Robin, he's getting sprung tomorrow. We should be on the road no later than ten in the morning. Can't wait to see you too. Here, she wants to talk to you."

"Hi Robin. Yes, in just a few hours, we'll be on our way. Huh? You do? What kind of surprise?" I asked as I looked over at Henry. He gave a look of mock terror and kept watching. "C'mon, no hints at all? Okay, guess we'll find out when we get there. Love you, too, here's Henry."

Henry grabbed the phone and yelled, "You better not be messin' with my chair, or our new home. Okay, yeah, love you too. See you tomorrow."

"You were a bit harsh with her, " I pointed out.

"I know, but she scares me when she starts her surprises."

"What could she have done that would be that bad?"

"I'm not trying to scare you, but once when I was away on assignment, just overnight, mind you, I returned home to a fuchsia bathroom."

"Fuchsia? In the bathroom?" Elliot echoed.

"Not in the bathroom, babe, it was the bathroom. Fuchsia walls, sink, tub, toilet, closet, window. It took me three months to get the window open, she'd used so many coats of paint."

"Wow, okay, maybe you should have been harsher with her. Henry, I don't want some ugly purple bathroom!"

"She promised we are going to love it. I guess no sense in borrowing trouble."

"Tomorrow, oh my God, I am so ready. And you, you must be so antsy needing to get to work again."

"I already did go back. Mr. Flanders said to write a human-interest story on my trip, so I've been sending him blurbs and he wants to make a serial out of them. Kind of a blog for the newspaper."

"Oh, so each week a new chapter is printed? That's brilliant on Mr. Flanders. Huge potential to expand readership. Hell, I may even buy a copy just to read it."

"You can have it for free. No need wasting money."

"Henry, you know what I like best about going home tomorrow?" Elliot shyly asked.

"What babe? Oh, no more Hurricane Hilda!"

"Ha Ha, yeah, but no. The best thing is we can sleep together and do whatever we want."

"It has been a long time," Henry agreed.

"Let's get to sleep so morning comes sooner. Night, Elliot," I said while kissing his cheek.

"Nighty night to you."

Chapter Eighteen
Home at Last

I was startled awake by something and instinctively turned towards my guy. Elliot was slightly turned on his right side, head resting on his pillow gently and breathing oh so softly. Steady, even breathing that lulled me back to sleep in contentment.

It felt as if I had only just closed my eyes a minute ago when I heard a voice from far away. It was yelling at me.

"Henry! Henry let's go. Time to get up and blow this popsicle stand!"

"Mm?"

"C'mon, Henry. I'll leave without you."

"Mm, what? Elliot is that you?" I said, groggily.

"No, it's the Cookie Monster, who do you think it is?"

"Sorry, sleepin'. What are you doing up in the middle of the night?"

"Open your eyes, sunshine. It's almost nine-thirty. Doc's been in, gave me my release papers, too."

"Man, did I conk out, jeez. I woke up in the night, straight out of a sound sleep, watched you sleeping soundly and that's the last I remember."

"You're okay though, aren't you? I don't want to go if you're not up to it."

"Are you serious? Wild horses couldn't stop me."

"Good, cuz we're going home!" Elliot said with a little dance.

"Give me five minutes to shower and dress."

"I'm feeling generous, take ten minutes."

I went in the bathroom with my heart full. Elliot was really happy.

After checking the room for stray items, we were making our way to the door when Nurse McFee arrived with the wheelchair. I could hear them talking softly and next I heard the nurse, "Hospital rules."

"Let's break em," Elliot challenged.

"No, that's one rule that stays in place," I said.

"Killjoy!"

"Yup that's me, Dr. Killjoy."

Elliot got to laughing so hard he had to sit down. I was thrilled to see him so elated.

"I see nothing funny, Mr. Scott, get in the chair," the nurse ordered.

Playtime apparently over, Elliot sullenly got in the chair while I grabbed all the bags. Getting off the elevator in the lobby, I said, "I'll go bring the car around."

"You should have done that before. Would have saved time, you know," Nurse Grump said as she glanced at her watch.

"If you're in a hurry, I can wait here by myself, you go on back in," Elliot suggested.

As I walked towards the car, I heard "Can't, it's against hospital rules."

Elliot's probably having a cow, I thought as I skillfully maneuvered through the lot. Elliot looked like a stuffed fish left on the shore too long.

"Let's get you in the car."

"Yeah, let us," Elliot said sharply.

After he was safely in the passenger seat, Nurse Mc Fee said, "Goodbye, safe drive." Then she turned and headed back through the automatic doors, just her and the wheelchair.

I hopped into the driver's seat, grabbed Elliot by the neck and pulled him into a warm, wet, tongue-filled kiss.

"Okay, I'm ready to go now, you?" I asked.

"Ah, yeah, um, yeah I'm ready, let's get outta here," Elliot agreed.

It took us most of the day to get back home. I didn't want to go too fast, and we ended up with a non-stress filled ride. It helped me to unwind after everything that happened to us. Elliot slept a lot during the trip. It was almost dark by the time, using my GPS and Robin, I was able to drive into our driveway, right up to the garage door.

Robin's car was suspiciously absent, and the house was bathed in a soft glow of light.

"Elliot, hey babe, we're home," I whispered in his ear.

"Home? Mm, Henry?"

"Right here, look," I gestured toward our home.

"Oh, it's so pretty. It looks like a fairy tale house. Let's get in there," Elliot rushed.

"Yes, let's. I'll grab the bags and –"

"No, just come in the house, babe."

"Okay with me." Getting out of the car, the distinct scent of the ocean permeated my nostrils. It was invigorating.

"Elliot do you – "

"Shh, listen," he said with his head cocked.

I held my breath and listened. I heard it; it was the sweet sound of the tide lapping the beach. Elliot and I stood in the driveway and leaned up against the car for a good three minutes, holding hands and listening to the ocean in the dark.

“I say we smell and listen again later, or we could open a window.”

“Well, aren’t we the smarty pants, c’mon, I do need to sit down.”

“I can take care of that, c’mere,” I scooped him up in my arms.

“Whoa, what are you doing?” Elliot squealed.

Once I got him completely in my arms, he stopped wiggling and wrapped his arms around my neck and melted into me.

I was a bit puzzled how to get in, as Robin would never have left the door unlocked. Then I remembered she used to leave a key under a heavy planter on her porch back years ago.

"Elliot, I gotta put you down a minute, babe."

"What's wrong? Too heavy for ya?"

"No, no nothing like that. I need to get the key from under the planter on the porch."

"We have a planter on our porch?"

"Yes, we do, thanks to Robin."

"Look, Henry. We also have a porch swing."

"So, I see. Wonder what else that girl's done."

I found the key under a huge cement pot. It was painted the same green as the house trim, but also had a circle of salmon around the opening. It held some kind of large fern.

"C'mere, I still want to carry you in."

"Okay, let's do it. That swing is beautiful, solid wood. I'm all yours, my love."

I picked him up once more and got us inside without any damage. I froze as I walked in. The foyer was bathed in soft light. That's when I saw the candles. Robin had skillfully placed battery-operated candles all over the room to give it a calming, magical feel.

"Wow," Elliot muttered. This is so where the tree is going!"

"Ha ha, good thinking, Elliot."

"Henry?" Elliot crooked next to me.

"Yes, dear?" I answered knowing I was about to give into something.

"Let's go find our bedroom," Elliot had a gleam in his eyes.

"We have no furniture. We'll have to sleep on the floor."

"I don't think so. I got a feeling our angel has set us up, I mean in a good way."

We left the downstairs behind and climbed a flight up to find our room. I found lots of things and then I opened the door near the end of the corridor and nearly fainted. "Elliot, come here, quick."

At my side in a flash, we both stood in awe. Elliot finally spoke. "You remember you told me once my bathroom wasn't a room, it was an experience?"

"Yeah, I remember."

"Well this isn't a bedroom, it's fuckin' Disneyland, man."

"Maybe Disney World too," I added.

"You may be right. This is the prettiest room I've ever seen."

"Me too," I agreed.

It had a huge California King straight ahead when walking in. To the left was a huge ceiling to floor electric fireplace with a cheery fire going. Also down that way was a private bathroom and large dressing area.

The bed, a four poster, was covered in a thick quilt. It was made up of a geometric pattern in blues, whites, yellows, and a small amount of salmon.

The bed had a small night table on each side with matching lamps on either side.

Elliot and I stood there, arms around each other, taking it all in.

"My brain seems to be only functioning at half speed."

"Mine, too," I said.

"What do ya think we ought to do?" My fiancé asked.

"Couple thoughts passed through me," I grinned.

"Yeah, I think I was having a couple of those thoughts myself," Elliot said back.

We turned towards each other slowly. We stood taking each other in.

"Elliot, your face is still beautiful. You have extra character now. But these eyes of sun," I said while kissing each lid, this skin, dipped in honey, your blonde curly mop, and most of all, that dimple that drives me wild," I said while kissing every inch of skin I could reach, especially his face. He needed to know he was going to be okay.

I knew I had him when he began to reciprocate. He kissed my neck and sucked on my earlobe.

"Bed," Elliot pulled me towards our own sanctuary in the middle of the room.

Once there, Elliot pushed me down flat and crawled on top of me while removing my clothes. I was having such a good time; I didn't realize I was totally naked, and he'd somehow gotten the lube and condoms from the drawer.

I was filling fast and reaching for him wherever I could snag a part of him. He was everywhere at once. I managed to get his jacket and shirt off and pulled him down close. I saw uncertainty in his eyes, that didn't turn to cockiness this time. Elliot's arm went around my neck and pulled me even closer. He responded to my kisses by licking my lips, then pushing into my mouth with that delicious tongue of his.

I readily gave permission to him by opening my mouth enough for him to enter. We fought over dominance of tongues and mouths.

Other areas of our bodies were also responding. With Elliot lying on top of me, I could feel his erection on my thigh. I wondered if he could feel mine.

"Mm um," was all I heard from Elliot, but it was enough to know he was happy. His head was on mine. I took his face in my hands and kissed it all over. I was rewarded with more happy grunts from him.

Elliot continued to kiss me all over, as his hands roamed up and down the naked skin where he'd just gotten my clothes off.

"Henry, you are so incredible. I could stay like this forever."

"Me too, babe."

"I wanna be inside you, babe." Elliot whispered in my ear with his hot breath.

"Yes, Elliot, yes. Do it."

He stared down at me with an evil glint in his eye for so long, it made me shiver. It also made me harder. He kissed, nipped, and sucked his way down to my cock and that drove me crazy. He grabbed a pillow and said," Lift your hips up."

I did and he slipped the pillow under my butt. I bent my knees and Elliot pushed them back to my chest. He proceeded to lube up his dick and then my opening with so much lube I thought maybe we should invest in the company.

Elliot bent forward and circled my mouth with his fingers. I understood and opened my mouth to him. After wetting his fingers, he reached down and eased one into my hole and twirled it around. I couldn't help but start to squirm. He next used two fingers and began to scissor inside me.

"Oh, babe. Oh, please."

"Someone's enjoying themselves," Elliot teased.

"Oh, you better believe it," I countered.

I felt much more pressure when the third finger went in, but it felt so good.

"Babe do me, please, I'm ready now."

"Yeah I think you are just about there."

Elliot took his fingers away and I was left cold and empty. I heard the lube top again and then he was back. He lubed his engorged cock once more, then lined up to my hole and entered me slowly so as not to hurt me.

"Wow, Henry, you feel so good, so tight. I could get very used to this."

"Me too, babe. You're so hot and big. Oh Elliot, I really love you."

" Love you too, Henry."

We watched each other and we both grabbed my dick at the same time. Laughing, I said " Great minds and all that."

"Oh Elliot, baby, I'm gonna explode any second."

"Oh, Henry, so am I. I'm so ready to, I'm gonna come."

Listening to him, I felt so close. Close to ejaculating and closer to Elliot.

"Oh, I'm ready, oh, oh Henry! Ahh."

"Elliot, that was, oh man, oh, ah, I'm coming."

We laid there, both panting loudly. My heart felt it would beat right out of my chest and reaching over to Elliot's chest, my hand moved with the beats. I reached down to pull up the bedding that had slid to the floor and yanked it all up to cover us. I then wrapped myself round his naked body and laid my head on his chest. He slid his back into me and took my arm. We were falling asleep when Elliot said, "Thank you for coming into my life, Henry."

"Thank you for taking me in, Elliot."

We fell into an exhausted sleep, and I had dreams I was floating on a marshmallow cloud.

I woke up slowly. Rising to consciousness, the scent of salty, sea air wafted through the air. My eyelids went up shakily like broken window shades. It took a moment to recall where I was. Seeing the full-length fireplace across the room, created a kaleidoscope of pleasant images from the past twelve hours. I turned my head to the left and beheld the most beautiful picture in the world.

Elliot, this miracle of a man. When I think back of how we met, I'm embarrassed. When I think of the last few hours, I'm elated.

I quietly slid out of bed and padded to the bathroom, our lovely bathroom with the garden tub. After taking care of business, I brushed my teeth and climbed back into bed.

Alone. I was all alone. Looking around, I noticed the French doors were a jar. Throwing my robe on, I instantly thought of our Vegas robes. I peeked out the door and there he stood, looking like Luke Skywalker staring at the twin suns of Tatooine.

I started out to him but got an idea. I silently closed the glass door, went downstairs to our gleaming kitchen, and started breakfast. I knew Robin would have fully stocked the fridge and the cupboards for us. I was soon frying the bacon I'd found in the fridge in a skillet I found in a cabinet. After the bacon, I got the eggs and toast started along with the coffee.

I located a serving tray on one of the granite countertops and began loading plates of food, orange juice, coffee, cream and sugar, plus napkins and eating utensils. I carried the whole thing up to our room. Sliding the tray on top of a bureau, I walked over and opened the French doors once more.

This time, he heard me.

"About time you got up, lazy bones. Come see this incredible view."

“I’ve seen the view. You come over here and kiss me properly, sir.”

“Very well, I’m coming.” As Elliot got closer, he began to sniff the air.

“Mm, something smells mighty good. We should go in and get something to eat.”

“I don’t see why we can’t have both, especially since the food is already

cooked and waiting for us.

“Waiting? You didn’t make reservations to some fancy place, did you?”

“That depends on how fancy a place you consider our home.”

“Our home? What are you – “

“Stay still for just a moment,” I said.

“Alright, but I am hungry. Hurry.”

I blew past him and got the tray from the bureau, sauntered out onto the balcony.”

“What is all this?”

“I made you breakfast. I thought we could eat out on the balcony.”

"Now there's a good idea, that's my fiancé, always thinking," Elliot said with a smile.

I got the tray and Elliot cleaned off the table and gathered a couple of chairs.

"Before we eat, let's go look at the only picture that moves." He was referring to our view and it was stunning. Elliot took me by the hand, and we stood at the banister and watched and listened to heavenly music. It came from the ocean and the seagulls. Then it was heard from somewhere just as heavenly to me, but him, not so much.

"Elliot, is that your stomach growling?" I teased.

"You know darn well it is, Henry."

"Let's get that tray out here and dig in. I think you'll enjoy what I made."

"I would eat tarpaper and nails if you told me you'd baked them yourself," Elliot laughed.

We sat on opposite sides of the round wicker table, eating, drinking our coffee and just living. I kept looking over at the porch swing and Elliot asked about it.

"I don't know, I guess the idea of having a big porch swing on the front porch, I never expected one outside our bedroom. I think Robin truly wanted to make this our sanctuary from the world."

"I got the same impression. You wanna go cuddle on the swing? It's looks really comfy with all of the padding and pillows."

"Yeah, I 'd love to," I returned.

We sauntered over to the swing, and I sat down. Elliot immediately snuggled against me with his head on my shoulder.

"I'm thinking three months."

"Um, three months for what, Elliot?"

"Our wedding. There are so many minute details to take care of and I really don't want to feel rushed. I'd also like to see if I can get hired for a movie, or a TV spot or something. That's on me, Henry. I really need to feel useful before I commit to us. Does that make any sense?"

"It makes perfect sense. You've got your phone; open Calendar and we'll pick a date."

"Oh, Henry, February twenty-second. It's a Tuesday, but the date is perfect."

"I love it, I absolutely love it. You wanna stay like this all day and make wedding plans and eat all the food up?"

"Sounds too good to be true, Henry. I'll grab some paper and a pen, and we can start planning. Robin's got the color schemes down. I think we're in charge of venue, here, and what to serve and I do have a thought about that. What if we did a brunch, with all kinds of pastries and doughnuts along with huge chafing dishes of eggs, bacon, sausages and hash browns as well."

"I think that's a marvelous idea and I'm sure Robin would help."

"I don't think you could stop that force of nature," Elliot approved.

"I think we should do a lot of this for the rest of our lives."

"Think up wedding plans?"

"No, you ding dong. Stay out here on our swing, watching and listening to nature."

"I have to agree with you, Elliot. Let's snuggle and cuddle and kiss and plan our wedding. We have the rest of our lives to be with each other. That thought makes me extremely happy."

"Me too, Henry. I love you."

"Love you, too, babe."

So, that's exactly what we did. We spent our weeks before the wedding talking, loving and appreciating each other and watching the ocean tide come in and go out every day.

The End

About the Author

Susan Quinn was born and raised in Massachusetts. She loved to make up stories when she was a child and she never quite lost the taste for it.

She started reading fanfiction stories of one of her favorite shows, Emergency! Reading the marvelous talent of so many writers, she began to concoct her own stories. A writer friend encouraged (pushed) her into publishing them and Susan now has several stories and a series to which she still receives kudos.

Susan soon decided to move on from fan fiction and write a novel. Sending it off to Nine Star Publishing, she was in total shock receiving the acceptance email on her birthday! Susan Quinn's first novel, A Reason for Tomorrow, will be released soon.

Susan Quinn continues to reside in Massachusetts with her twenty-six-year-old son. Her husband passed away in May 2018 after a lengthy battle with metastasized colon cancer.

Like most human beings, Susan Quinn is a plethora of contradictions. Two of her favorite shows are Criminal Minds and The

Partridge Family. She loves movies from the thirties to the sixties, and yet enjoys the newest movie on HBO. Susan loves a light comedy like Mom and watched every episode of The Newsroom.

Wine is an essential food group and must be white, never red. White zin is her favorite, but why is it dark pink?

Susan Quinn's goal in life is to honor her late husband who was a constant source of strength and encouragement. Also, for the public to have an interesting story to read.

Read more at https://susanquinnauthor.com.